# The
# RABBIT
## Girl

# RABBIT
## girl

## Mary Arrigan

**F**

FRANCES LINCOLN
CHILDREN'S BOOKS

First published in Great Britain and the USA in 2011 by
Frances Lincoln Children's Books, 4 Torriano Mews,
Torriano Avenue, London NW5 2RZ
www.franceslincoln.com

A catalogue record for this book is available from the British Library.

ISBN: 978-1-84780-156-2

Set in Palatino

Printed in Croydon, Surrey, UK by CPI Bookmarque Ltd. in January 2011

135798642

*For Cuiva,*
*and in memory of Bert Hewson,*
*antique dealer and gentleman*

# CHAPTER ONE

## IRELAND, 1934

'That's not my mam!' protested the five-year-old boy, shrinking behind the elderly woman's ample skirt.

She drew him out firmly by the arm. 'It *is* your mam, Tony. Now, you come over here and kiss her goodbye, there's a good lad.'

Tony clung to Mrs Mooney's skirt, turning his head away from the figure lying on the bed. That yellow face did not belong to his mam. His mam had rosy cheeks, and eyes that laughed when she was telling him stories about people with strange names who lived in faraway lands filled with caves, castles, ogres and animals that could talk. It was that memory which Tony clung to in this bedroom, transformed from its warm cosiness into a place that smelled of medicine and starchy bed linen folded in mothballs. Candles around the bed sputtered in the breeze blowing up the stairs from the open front door. All Mam's comforting clutter had been hidden away. Even the picture of rabbits in a field was covered with a white cloth.

'We'll go there,' Mam used to say. 'You and me, Tony, we'll go there and play with those rabbits.'

*Maybe that's where Mam is*, thought the little boy. *Maybe she's gone to play with the rabbits and is waiting for me.* He tried to pull away from Mrs Mooney's grasp. She dragged him over to the bed, but all the while he kept his head averted, eyes focused on the borrowed crucifix standing on the bedside table.

'Jesus will help her,' his dad had said when he put the cross there. 'Jesus will make your mam better.'

'Now,' Mrs Mooney said, lifting Tony up. 'You kiss your mam goodbye.'

She thrust his face against the stone-cold cheek of the figure on the bed. Tony struggled, but Mrs Mooney held him there.

The figure's lips were pressed tightly together, its eyes shut. Its head was covered in a white cloth, making it look like a wax nun. This was not his mam.

But when he saw the bloodless fingers entwined in his mother's blue rosary beads, he knew. His hopeless wail echoed around the walls of the small house, and the gathered neighbours crossed themselves. Tony turned his face away, and was again confronted by the crucifix.

'Jesus didn't make Mam better,' he sobbed, lashing out at it. Mrs Mooney caught his wrist before he could sweep the cross off the table.

'You little rascal,' she whispered, still holding the boy's wrist. 'But, sure, you're not thinking right, you poor little mite.'

Later, Tony stood with his father at the bottom of the stairs near the front door, as men in black eased the coffin down the narrow stairs.

*Bump, thud, grunt, thud.* Not nice noises. There should not be noises like that when they were carrying Mam. She wouldn't like it. Tony buried his face in his father's new overcoat and tried to think of Mam in a field with rabbits, and not in that bumpy box.

Every Sunday after that, Tony and his father took flowers to Mam's grave. Then his father had to go away. Lots of men on the street went away. Mrs Mooney said it was because the shoe factory had closed down and they had to look for work somewhere else. Tony didn't like staying in Mrs Mooney's house. He wanted his father to come and take him away. Every day he stood at the front door, scanning the street for the familiar figure to appear.

'Best get away from that door, lad,' Mrs Mooney said. 'He'll come for you when he finds work. The two of you will live in a grand house and you can have a hutch for those rabbits you're always going on about.'

Tony flinched. Rabbits were a sore point between himself and Mrs Mooney.

It had begun the day Joe Dolan from the cottages knocked at the door. He was carrying a long stick from which five dead rabbits were hanging. Mrs Mooney had been pleased to see him and gave him a shilling for two of the rabbits.

'Rabbit stew,' she smiled at Tony, as she plonked the limp creatures on the kitchen table.

'They're dead,' he said, shocked. 'The rabbits are dead.'

'Of course they're dead, child,' Mrs Mooney laughed. 'How else could we eat them? Joe here is an expert rabbit-trapper. Keeps me in cheap meat. I can't afford beef or bacon. Isn't that right, Joe?'

Joe nodded, giving the boy a meaningful scowl.

'Sure, you've been eating my rabbit stew ever since you came here,' went on Mrs Mooney.

'No,' wailed Tony. 'I didn't. I couldn't.'

'Ah, but you did, and you could,' laughed Mrs Mooney. 'And we'll be having it again this evening with carrots and potatoes.'

'Not me,' said Tony, backing away. 'Not ever.'

And he didn't. He stubbornly refused rabbit under any guise or name. Mrs Mooney tried calling her rabbit stew 'Brown Broth', 'Mooney Mash' and 'Carrot Surprise', but Tony always detected the rabbit meat and kept his lips tightly closed.

'Ye little upstart,' Mrs Mooney said. 'Ye can just starve, for all I care.'

But she did care enough to buy eggs for her awkward charge. 'And nothing died for this meal,' she told him, as she served him his daily fried egg and potato.

But word of Tony's problem with rabbits reached the school yard, and he suffered teasing and bullying that left him lying awake at nights. At first he tried to explain to his tormentors that his mam had gone to a field of rabbits and was going to take him there too. But they only laughed.

*Sissy*, they called him. *Bunny baby. Whingey Mollie.* And, worst of all, *Snotty-face.* The tough Dolan brothers often lay in wait for him on his way home from school and beat him up – with promises of instant death if he told on them.

Mrs Mooney was sometimes annoyed at the state of the boy's clothes. But Tony kept his silence and took the blame for his torn jumper and bloody nose.

'I fell,' he'd say.

If Mrs Mooney suspected any rough stuff, she simply tut-tutted. Her own sons had grown up fighting their corner. It was something boys had to learn to cope with. Good for them. Made them tough.

So Tony learned how to play truant, disappearing into the streets after setting out for school and coming back at three o'clock.

When two letters arrived together one morning, Mrs Mooney opened the one with the English stamp first.

'Thank God,' she said. 'Your father is coming to collect you.' She looked at Tony over her reading glasses. 'I don't know who's more pleased,' she chuckled, 'me or you.'

'Will we go back to our own house now?' the child asked. Mrs Mooney drew him to her. 'Not really, lad,' she said gently. 'England. Your daddy is taking you to live in England.'

So the second letter, which was from the headmaster complaining about Tony's absences, somehow didn't matter any more.

# CHAPTER TWO

# ENGLAND,
# THE PRESENT DAY

Mallie Kelly turned the key in the front door and was knocked back by a strong smell of spray polish and floor cleaner. The house was looking far too neat. *Oh-oh.* That meant Mum was on a 'homey' binge, frantically cleaning to make up for another job loss. Why had she got the push this time? For scribbling pictures of mice and rabbits on office paper? Rude cartoons of the boss?

'Cutbacks,' her mum said bitterly, slapping the arm of the sofa and coughing through the cloud of dust that rose up. 'Last in, first out.'

'Hell, Mum,' said Mallie.

'Don't swear,' sighed her mum. 'You just make sure you don't end up like me – almost forty and nothing to show for it. Except for you, my love,' she added. 'Put on the kettle, Mal. We'll have a cuppa and you can cheer me up.'

Mallie shook her head. 'What can I say that'll cheer you up? Say we've won the lottery? Dream on, Mum. Maybe I could get a part-time job. If I pile my hair up, I can look sixteen…'

'Hold it right there, young lady. You'll do no such thing,' said her mum, throwing a clean rug over the sagging sofa. 'You'll concentrate on school and rise above this ghastly scenario.'

Mallie put her hands to her head. 'Ever heard of *now*, Mum? We need cash now. What's the harm in doing a bit of part-timing…?'

'No, Mal,' put in her mum. 'Please. We've already had that discussion and the answer is still no. Now, stand clear, this spray is full of toxins, but it sure shifts the grot. And,' she added, 'don't give me any whys or wherefores about my job. I was just unlucky.'

❧❧❧

'If only she could find work that suits her,' Mallie groaned to her friend Jamila that evening, as they walked through the shopping centre. 'Something she could do from home at her own pace. My mum is an "I don't do rules" type of person.'

'Oh, Mal,' said Jamila. 'My grandfather once told me about the trouble *he* had when he first came over from India. He said you never get over the hurt of rejection when you're looking for work. Be patient with your mum – you're all she's got.'

'I suppose so,' agreed Mallie. 'If only she'd get back to painting! But her art just doesn't sell.'

'I'm not surprised,' said Jamila. 'Honestly, Mal, from what I've seen, it's a bit slap-happy.'

'Say what you really mean, Jam,' Mallie laughed. 'They're more Virgin-Mary-meets-meat-grinder. She used to do such great, realistic stuff, especially animals. But now she reckons that's outdated – hasn't slapped anything on canvas for ages. So it's back to the job centre, and small ads in the local paper again.' She sighed.

'Your mum needs male company,' Jamila said, as they grabbed two seats outside Bob's Nice Ices. 'Otherwise you'll never get away with me and backpack around the world, and become celebs when we're eighteen. You'll be stuck in your semi-detached, making cocoa for your old mum and going to Bingo with her on Friday nights. No, Mal, romance is your answer. A middle-aged guy who has money and his own teeth, and you'd be right off the hook.'

'Nice thought,' said Mallie with a laugh, counting out the money for a mint choc. 'If a bit old-fashioned. You read too many of your aunty's old Mills and Boon books, Jam. Down-at-heel-heroine-meets-macho-aristocrat-who-sweeps-her-off-her-feet sort of stuff.'

'Nothing old-fashioned about a bit of romance,' retorted Jamila, going in to order the ices.

*Perhaps Jamila is right,* mused Mallie, thinking of her mother's face framed by its wild hair dyed several shades of red. *Maybe a bit of romance would brighten her life.*

Things had been OK when Mum's partner, Simon, was around to organise their lives and help foot the bills. But he had skipped off to Amsterdam on a business trip two years ago and hadn't been seen since.

'Maybe I'll try painting again, Mal,' said her mum later. 'Big landscapes. Exhibit them in the library. Surely people would like colourful landscapes.

11

People who read usually like pictures. It goes with the imaginative side of the brain.'

'Or maybe try something different, Mum. Your old style.'

'Why?'

Mallie shrugged. 'Something smaller and simpler, maybe? Like you used to do. Animals, people. You know, proper stuff…'

'People like colours, Mallie. It puts a little bit of cheer into their drab lives.'

Mallie shook her head. What was the point in arguing?

'What can I buy her, Jamila?' Mallie asked, on the way home from school the next day. 'What can you buy a mum who's hit forty and is miserable about it?'

'How much money do you have?' asked Jamila. 'Enough for a bit of jewellery? Jewellery is happy stuff, Mal. That's what my mum tells my dad, and it works every time.'

'Yeah, sure, Jam,' said Mallie. 'I've enough to buy a diamond bracelet, and, of course, the matching tiara for the cocktail parties… Get real, Jam. The only jewellery I could afford would come out of a Christmas cracker.'

'No need to bite my head off,' said Jamila. 'You asked for advice and I'm giving it.'

'Sorry. Didn't mean to snap,' muttered Mallie. 'Put it down to desperation. I've got to get a job. Something after school – and it has to be a secret from Mum. She'd go mad.'

'That's the start of the slippery slope,' laughed Jamila.

'What do you mean?'

'Keeping secrets from your mum. Next, you'll be downing cans of beer and hanging out with low life. I can see it all in the tabloids: *Teenage ASBO jailed for disruptive behaviour in squat*. *"It all began when I started keeping secrets from my mum," she confessed.'*

'You're mental,' said Mallie. 'And anyway, I already hang out with low life.'

'Huh?'

'You! Come on, let's mosey round town.'

'I have to pick up some pet food for my brother's rabbit,' said Jamila. 'Can't see why *I* have to do it, though. Lazy thing. Just sits around flopping his big ears. Useless. The rabbit is pretty useless too.'

By the time Mallie had started to laugh, Jamila was striding ahead, her black plait bouncing at each step. As they approached the pet shop, they were surprised to see a small crowd outside. Jamila stopped, and Mallie caught up with her.

'What's going on ?' she asked.

'Maybe it's some big star buying a pink poodle for her handbag,' replied Jamila, who forever lived in hope of running into a celebrity and forging a lifelong friendship that would gain her entry into the world of paparazzi and stretch limos.

'Well if that's the case, why are they all laughing? You don't laugh at big stars, Jam. You go gobsmacked. That's not a gobsmacked crowd.'

When they reached the shop window, it became clear what was causing the laughter. A tall, harassed-looking man was trying to coax a spitting kitten from a rail above the window, and not having much success. He had already spilt a pan of water and upset several bowls of food. He stretched out a pole with a net at the end. The kitten spat, and swiped at the net. The man stumbled against the partition between the window and the shop floor, sending it flying. Several puppies yelped with delight and escaped from their enclosure. The crowd laughed. The man jumped about, trying to round up the puppies.

'A side-show!' laughed Jamila. 'This is better than … hey, Mallie! Where are you going?' she called, as her friend vanished into the shop.

**CHAPTER THREE**

Mallie pushed past the man as another puppy slipped from his grasp.

'Wrong, wrong. You're doing this all wrong,' she said. 'You have to keep calm.'

With that, she sat down on the floor and eased her hands towards the three wayward pups. Curious, they approached her. One by one, Mallie lifted them into her arms and stroked them. They licked her face and playfully pulled at the buttons of her jacket.

The man scratched his head. 'Amazing,' he said. 'I don't suppose you could get that kitten, while you're at it?'

Mallie handed him the three puppies and climbed up into the window. With the same easy coaxing, she soon got the kitten down on to her arm and whispered to it as she cuddled it. A cheer went up from the onlookers.

Jamila watched with amazement from the doorway.

'Cool, Mallie,' she said. 'What will you do for an encore? Anything else you could charm – apart from him over there?' she added in a whisper.

'As you say – cool,' said the man, as he took the kitten from Mallie. 'Thanks a lot. My assistant has left and I'm trying to manage on my own. Not very well, I'm afraid,' he added sheepishly. 'I think I might have panicked a bit. Let me treat you to a free kitten. You look like a girl who loves animals.'

'No, thanks,' said Mallie. 'Mum won't let me have a pet. She used to say it was hard enough keeping the house civilised, without having a dumb animal messing it up as well – and that was just her ex-partner,' she added, with a self-conscious laugh.

'Well, let me offer you a glass of juice,' the man said. 'It's the least I can do for someone who's done me a big favour.'

'Ooh, lovely,' said Jamila, before Mallie could refuse.

Mallie nudged her friend in the ribs as they followed the man into a small space behind the shop.

'Don't push it, Jam,' she whispered. 'It was no big deal rounding up a couple of puppies.'

'It's good manners to let people show gratitude, Mal.'

Mallie smiled. Jamila always seemed to have the right answer.

'The shop is really my father's,' the man was saying, as he poured apple juice from a carton. 'He's in a convalescent home at the moment, recovering from a broken leg.'

'Chasing puppies, was he?' asked Jamila.

The man laughed. Mallie noticed that his green eyes crinkled when he laughed, and his hair was cut tight and flecked with grey – the sort of man who'd take his kids bowling and to pantomimes. Mallie sniffed away the thought as sentimental slush. She'd had it with fathers, thank you. Her real father had died when she was small, and her other so-called 'step-father' had done a bunk.

'No,' the man replied to Jamila's question.

'He fell off the pavement while he was out jogging.'

'Jogging?' said Jamila.

The man laughed again. 'I know what you're thinking. If he's father to someone my age, then he must be antediluvian.'

'Anti what?'

'Not anti, it's ante,' put in Mallie. 'Antediluvian with an e. Means 'old'. Before the Flood.'

'What flood?' asked Jamila.

'It's an Old Testament thing,' said Mallie. 'It means before the time of Noah.'

'Noah? The one with the beard, the ark and the animals two-by-two?'

'Yes, Jam. Him.'

'Anyway,' went on the man, 'I came back to look after things while he's away.'

'Back from where?' asked Jamila,

'That's none of our business,' whispered Mallie. She wanted to finish her drink and go. But Jamila was just settling in.

'From Australia,' the man replied. 'I've been in Oz for the past ten years.'

'Australia! said Jamila. 'Me and Mallie are going to do the world when we're eighteen. What were you doing there? Bushwhacking? Backpacking?'

'Animal research,' the man replied, refilling Jamila's glass. 'It's what I do.' He laughed, when he saw their surprised expressions. 'I study animals.'

'Pardon me,' said Mallie with a smile, 'but I hope you handle them better than that lot in the shop.'

The man laughed. *'Touché.* Give me a croc or a kangaroo any day – they're a doddle compared to a spitting kitten or a slithery puppy. Anyway, sorry to rush you girls, but I'd better get back to running the shop.'

'Wait!' exclaimed Jamila, almost spilling her drink with excitement. 'Did you say you have no assistant?'

The man nodded. 'Upped sticks and left me in the lurch. Said he'd got a job in a burger joint – and that he'd sooner handle dead meat that goes between buns than live meat that bites.'

'That's horrible,' said Mallie.'

'You've said it!' said the man. 'Better off without him – even if it means me running ragged trying to run this place on my own...'

'That's what I'm talking about!' Jamila was waving her hand. 'Mallie here is looking for a job! Part-time. After school.'

'Jamila!' Mallie hissed. 'I'll strangle you, I really

will. With your own best scarf to make it extra painful.'

'Think about it,' Jamila went on, leaning closer to her friend. 'A couple of hours after school. You'd be made, Mallie. And you could get your mum that prezzie and still have a bit of money for yourself. Miss Independence. Besides, you love all that animal stuff. I've seen your bedroom walls with those pictures your mum drew for you when you were little – in the days when she did *real* art.'

'Stop right there,' said Mallie with a scowl. Having the private contents of her bedroom paraded before a stranger was, she thought, a step too far.

'It's true,' went on Jamila. 'You're animal-mad.' She turned towards the man.

'How about it?'

'Don't mind my friend,' said Mallie. 'She gets ideas she can't control. Thanks for the juice. Come on, Jamila.'

The man scratched his head. 'It would certainly get me out of a spot,' he said. 'A couple of hours a week – maybe an hour or so Wednesday to Friday and a few hours on Saturday. Until I get a full-time assistant. I'd be really grateful. And I can see that you're well qualified,' he added, with a smile.

'Go for it, Mal,' whispered Jamila. 'Minutes ago you were moaning because you've no money. Here's a job – kittens and cuddly puppies – just your sort of thing.'

'I just – I need to think about it, that's all,' said Mallie.

'You're absolutely right,' said the man. 'Take your time. Discuss it with your parents and you can tell me tomorrow – OK? Here,' he went on, reaching across an untidy desk, 'here's my card, or rather, my father's card. My name is Steve. Call me tomorrow and let me know if you want the job.'

Farther down the street, the two girls stopped to read it.

'A.P. Armstrong,' said Jamila. 'Nice name, Armstrong. Macho. Are you going take the job?'

Mallie turned the card over thoughtfully. She frowned. Then she smiled.

'Of course I will – but not because you suggested it,' she added. 'I just needed time to think.'

'Great, Mal,' laughed Jamila. 'Will you tell your mum?'

Mallie shook her head. 'What do you think?'

Jamila made a face. 'Nah,' she said. 'She'd fuss.'

'Exactly. She won't even notice if I'm home a

couple of hours late. She'll think I'm with you. And you'd better back me up.'

'You're asking me to lie?' said Jamila. 'Oh my, pushing the boundaries of friendship...'

'Yes, well, it was your idea. Besides, you owe me for prattling on about my bedroom walls. Do that again, and you're dead.'

'Sorry,' said Jamila. 'Anyway, you're sorted. I'm really pleased. See? With your earnings and the money I earn on Sunday mornings from working in my dad's shop, we'll be equal. We can do Boots' cosmetic counter together.'

'Yes. Sorted.'

'Great,' said Jamila. She looked thoughtful. 'By the way,' she said, 'how long has it been since your father ran off?'

'Stepfather,' put in Mallie. 'And he wasn't even that, really. Mum and he didn't marry. They were just partners.'

'Whatever,' said Jamila. 'How long?'

'Two years. And I don't want to talk about it, if you don't mind.'

'I know, I know,' said Jamila. 'Sorry, Mal. But this is Jamila here – your best friend, with your interests at heart. I'm telling you, your mum needs a man in her life. She's not getting any younger and you don't want her to turn into a bitter old hag. Do you want her to make your life miserable – to have you dressing in tweed and working in a safe, boring job, then running home to look after her when her knees give up?'

'What are you getting at, Jamila?' Mallie asked suspiciously. 'You're starting to scare me.'

'Sorry, Mal,' said Jamila. 'I get this from my Gran. We talk a lot. She tells me how things were in India long ago. She had a pretty rough time when my grandpa died. He was killed when he fell from an overcrowded train.'

'Oh, that's awful, Jam,' said Mallie.

'Well, I never actually met him. Still, it was rough on Gran. Now she's always saying that happiness is a precious thing and that we should try to help others be happy too.'

'And my mum is on your list? Get real, Saint Jamila,' laughed Mallie. 'You're going soft.'

'No,' insisted Jamila. 'It's not healthy for a woman to be living without a bit of romance. She needs a man in her life: someone to take her out, make her feel good.'

'Yes,' agreed Mallie. 'So?'

'You're not picking up my train of thought, are you, Mallie? He'd do.' She nodded back towards the pet shop. 'He's dishy, for an older guy.'

Mallie laughed. 'Give it a rest, Jam. You want me to push this guy on my mum just because he works with small animals? I don't think so.'

'Just help it along a bit. Look,' said Jamila patiently, 'my other grandparents – Dad's parents – their marriage was arranged. They didn't meet until their wedding. And they ended up totally dedicated to one another.'

'Don't tell me,' said Mallie. 'Your granny hopped on to your grandad's funeral pyre, she loved him so much.'

'Don't be coarse, Mallie Kelly. Anyway, they're both alive and kicking and running a restaurant in Hounslow. I'm merely pointing out that people can be gently pushed into companionship that could develop into a happy-ever-afterness. Think of it. Can't you see your mum's eyes brighten as she gets ready for a night out?'

Mallie frowned. 'Forget it, Jam. Mum won't even know I'm working for this guy. They'll never meet.'

'So you're happy to let your ageing mum go on to be a lonely old has-been?'

Mallie thought for a moment. Mum lonely? Yes, Jamila was right there. All Mum ever did was look for jobs, get sacked, go into deep depressions and spend her evenings watching *Coronation Street* and re-runs of old comedies. And, when her self-esteem sank even lower, making half-hearted trips to the gym with some of her weight-obsessed cronies. Not much of a life.

'I like your mum. She deserves better,' put in Jamila. 'And you're my best friend. What's there to lose?'

'Don't go on about it, Jamila,' said Mallie. 'I've just decided to help out in a pet shop for a few hours – and already you're marrying off my mother.'

# CHAPTER FOUR

## LONDON, 1935

Tony peered down into the dark water on either side of the gangplank, *slap slap*, like a monster licking its lips, waiting for someone to fall off the flimsy wooden bridge and be gobbled up. His father held his hand tightly and guided him aboard the mailboat. The Kingstown quay below was crowded with people seeing off relations and friends who were on their way across the Irish Sea to England. Nobody came to see off Tony and his father because they'd had to come to Kingstown the night before, armed with Mrs Mooney's sandwiches and medals of Saint Christopher to keep them safe on their journey.

'He'll keep that big tub of a ship from sinking,' Mrs Mooney had said.

Tony fingered the medal that she'd pinned to his pullover and hoped that this saint would do his job better than Jesus, who had been supposed to cure Mam.

'Say goodbye to Ireland,' said his father, lifting the boy up so that he'd have a better view of the receding coastline. 'And hello, world,' he added in a whisper.

Somebody started to play a mouth organ and people joined in singing. Later, as the ship got under way, there was dancing on deck. When it got dark and the sea became rockier, there was a dash for seats inside. Tony vomited up Mrs Mooney's sandwiches and the chocolate his father had bought him. The smell remained on his clothes for the remainder of the journey because the rest of their belongings were packed in the hold. Tony was sick twice more until there was nothing left in his stomach, and his father said that maybe his brains might come next. He laughed as he said it, but Tony kept his hands on his head after that, just in case.

At Holyhead, the tired and crumpled travellers disembarked and boarded a bus.

'Is this it?' the smelly, worn-out child asked.

'Are we here now, Daddy?'

'Not too far, son. This is Wales. We go through Wales for a while, and then we'll be in England.'

'Will that be soon?'

'Soon enough, lad. Lie back now, and get some sleep.'

But sleep only made Tony feel sicker when he woke up. Mrs Mooney had said that he'd be in his nice new home with hutches for rabbits in no time at all. But there seemed to be a lot of time, and it wasn't very nice. However, with his father's arm around him, he eventually fell into a deep slumber.

He awoke, bleary-eyed, when his father nudged him gently. 'London, Tony.' he said. 'We're in London.'

Tony looked with amazement at all the high buildings and busy streets. How would they find their way through all these rushing people and dangerous-looking carriages that had sparks coming from a rod running along wires overhead?

'They're trams, Tony,' his father said.

Tony shrank back when his father tried to take him aboard one of them.

'Don't worry,' his father laughed, lifting him. 'This will take us right to our door.'

*Right to our door?* Did this mean that trams, with

sparks and clanking wheels, would be passing their door every day? That was a scary thought. Tony gave his father a bewildered look. A stout woman on the other side of the aisle looked at Tony and sniffed, then leaned away.

'We've been travelling all night,' his father explained. But the woman pursed her lips and wrinkled her nose.

'Snobby cow,' Tony's father whispered, and giggled. Tony giggled too, even though he didn't know what 'snobby' meant.

The tram rumbled through endless streets before stopping at a row of grey, dingy buildings.

'We're here!' said Tony's father.

Tony looked up at the high buildings that towered over him. He wondered how people could live so high up. How would they get the turf up there for their winter fires? Did they have outdoor lavatories – did they have to dash down all those steps whenever they wanted to have a wee?

His father stopped outside a tall, narrow house with one set of steps up to the peeling front door, and another leading down to a basement. An old woman was sitting on the top step, knitting something red. She smiled a toothless smile and nodded at the two of them.

'Brought the prodigal here, then?' she asked.

'I have indeed,' smiled Tony's father. 'Say hello to Mrs Carter, Tony.'

Tony shrank closer to his father as the old woman reached out a gnarled hand and patted his head.

'Grand pair of eyes,' she said. 'Welcome to Waterloo House,' she added, with a chuckle. 'Or should I say Waterloo Tenement?' Then she resumed her knitting. Tony wondered what a tenement was, as he followed his father up stone stairs and past several doors from which he could hear the sounds of crying babies and muffled voices. There was a smell of cooking mixed with the strong disinfectant smell of cinema lavatories back home. Tony sniffed, and made a face.

'At least it's a clean smell,' his father laughed.

Higher they climbed, his father's heavy boots clomping rhythmically on the worn steps. At last he stopped outside a shabby green door.

'Home, Tony,' his father smiled, as he put the key in the lock. 'Our own London home.'

Tony stood in the doorway and shifted from one foot to the other as he took everything in. At the far end, two long windows looked out on grey buildings across the street. Tucked into a corner of the room was a brass bed strewn with discoloured blankets. A big sink with a dripping tap stood near a cooker; pots and pans were piled on the floor beside it. A small table covered in oilcloth was set with two enamel mugs and plates. One of the spindly chairs on either side of the table had a cushion on it. Tony knew that was his place. But he didn't want it to be his place – he didn't want anything to be labelled 'his' because that would mean staying here for ever. The only familiar things were the empty packs of Wild Woodbine cigarettes strewn in the black iron fireplace. Mam used to complain about them at home.

His heart leapt when he saw a photo of Mam standing on the mantlepiece beside a tin of pencils, a bundle of letters, a candle ('in case the electricity goes,' his father said later), and a dog-eared photograph of Laurel and Hardy. He had often gone to the cinema to see those two with Mam and Daddy. Mam would nudge him as she shook with laughter. It made him feel all the more lonely, seeing her photo up there.

'What's that smell?' Tony asked. He was still standing by the door. He remembered Mam's words once as she told him a bedtime story. 'Princes and heroes,' she had said, 'never rush foolishly into trouble. They go to meet it with caution.'

Tony's father patted the boy's shoulder. 'Still worried about the smell, Tony? It's gas. It leaves a funny sort of smell. You'll get used to it.'

But Tony shook his head. He'd never get used to anything in this high place with no yard.

'Why is there a bed in the living-room?' he asked.

His father laughed. 'Everything is in the living-room, son. This room is our home. Let's go in.' He half-pushed the reluctant boy inside and closed the door behind them. 'Home,' he said again.

Tony caught his breath. This wasn't home. This wasn't the fine house with a garden for a rabbit hutch that Mrs Mooney had told him about.

Outside, somebody shouted and there was the echoing slam of a door. Father and son looked at one another. 'You'll get used to that, too,' said his father gently. 'Now, take off that smelly coat and we'll get you cleaned up.'

Tony shrank back. If he took off his coat, it would mean he was stuck here.

'Where's the lav, Daddy?' he asked.

'Just down the hall, son,' his father replied. 'I'll show you. We share with a few neighbours,' he added. 'Bring some of those old newspapers with you. You can tear them into squares.'

There were two women standing outside the lavatory door. Both of them were smoking cigarettes, the smoke curling up over scarves tied around their heads like turbans. Tony had once seen a picture in a book Mam had about an eastern prince who wore a scarf like that. *Scheherazade*, the book was called. The scarf story was about a princess who told story after story to her evil husband the prince. Mam told Tony that the prince kept marrying women and then killing them – apart from Scheherazade, because she went on telling him stories. Tony had had nightmares for ages afterwards, and Mam had to remind him that it was only a story.

But these women weren't in a story. They were real, in this strange, grey place. Perhaps they were related to the evil prince. That made Tony even more nervous. What do you say to people who wear the same headgear as an eastern prince who kills people? Would he have enough stories to keep him alive, if the women picked on him? He didn't like this place at all. More than anything, he wanted to go back home to familiar things. He clutched his father's hand tightly.

One of the women nodded to Tony's father.

'Been over for the boy, then, have you?' she asked. 'How do you like England?' she asked, leaning towards Tony.

Tony moved closer to his father. The woman spoke with a funny accent and she had smoky breath.

'Don't worry, love,' laughed the other woman. 'We don't bite. Better get out of that smelly coat, though, or we shall have to hose you down, eh?'

'Say hello to Doris and Jenny,' said Tony's father, easing him gently towards the women. 'You'll soon get to know them.'

Tony didn't want to get to know them. When they said he could use the lavatory before they did, he went in and bit his lip to keep from crying out. He should be happy now; he was with his daddy again. But all he could think of was that funny gas smell in the room at the top of all those steps and the greyness outside the window. A room with no view of the sky and no escape. And women with turbans, who were like a killer prince.

'Can we go home now?' he asked his father later. 'I've seen England, Daddy. Let's go home.'

His father put his hands on the boy's shoulders and stooped to look into his eyes.

'This is it, Tony,' he said. 'We're here to stay. It's not so bad, really. You'll make friends.'

'I don't want friends. I want to go home.'

'This is where my work is, Tony,' his father said softly. 'You remember how the shoe factory closed down?' Tony nodded. 'Well I couldn't get work at home. That's why I had to come here. I have a job now. That's why I went home for you. We can be a family again, you and me.'

'I don't like this place,' Tony tried not to sound whiney. Only cowards whined – the Dolans had said so. 'It's smothery.'

'I know,' admitted his father. 'But when I have enough money, we'll move to a real house with a garden. '

'And a rabbit hutch?'

His father laughed. 'Of course, with a rabbit hutch. And white rabbits. None of your common brown fellows.'

Tony cheered up enough to take off his smelly coat. 'OK,' he said. 'I'll stay, then.'

# CHAPTER FIVE

'Hey, Mal. Ready for a bit of Saturday shopping?'

Mallie looked up from cleaning the hamster cage. Two weeks had passed and she had settled into an easy routine working for Steve Armstrong. She'd got used to parting with cuddly pets, and had stopped trying to put people off buying the animals she liked best.

Mallie placed the hamsters gently in the cage. 'See you, fellas,' she said.

'How do you know?' asked Jamila, peering in at the furry creatures as they burrowed about in fresh wood shavings.

'How do I know what?'

'That they're fellas.'

'Because I look,' said Mallie. 'Would you like to see?' she went on, opening the lid of the cage.

'No, ta,' said Jamila, putting her hand on the lid and closing it down again. 'I can think of better things than looking at hamsters' bums. Come on, let's get out of here. Good shopping time wasted. Anyway, you want to get that present for your mum, remember? I'll help you choose.'

'That's what I'm afraid of,' laughed Mallie. 'You'll talk me into buying something weird.'

'*Moi*?' said Jamila with mock dismay.

At a respectable distance from the shop, Mallie counted her first fortnightly pay packet.

'Wow,' said Jamila, peering over her shoulder. 'All that, for working a few hours. Cool, Mallie. And your mum doesn't suspect?'

'So far, so good. She thinks I'm either doing extra stuff at school or else hanging out with you. No problem. Not even on Saturdays. I feel guilty. No, I don't,' she added hastily. 'What's there to be guilty about, for heaven's sake? I'm a woman of independent means.'

'Right. Now, let's start looking for jewellery.'

The jeweller's proved a disappointment. When the girls read the price-tags, Mallie's pay packet faded to insignificance.

'Hell, Jamila,' groaned Mallie. 'I couldn't even afford one fiddly little earring, never mind the pair.'

'Does it have to be jewellery?' asked Jamila.

Mallie shrugged. 'What else is there? Chocolates? She'd get fat and blame me.'

'Flowers?' offered Jamila.

'They die. I want something she'll remember always. You have to have something to remember when you get a nought in your age. Remember telling me about being ten, and throwing a tantrum when you were taken to your mum's favourite restaurant?'

'Don't remind me,' muttered Jamila. 'I was expecting a bike. What about second-hand jewellery?'

'Cast-off trinkets? I don't think so.'

'No, hold on,' put in Jamila. 'Antique shops sometimes do something cheaper than places like this.'

Mallie mulled over this. 'No harm in having a look, I suppose. Come on.'

Bert's Antiques & Bric-a-Brac was down a side street, its swinging sign creaking gently in the wind.

A bell jangled as the two girls entered, and a stout man loomed up from behind a beaded curtain. The smoke from the cigarette in the corner of his mouth had left a yellow streak in his grey hair.

'Ladies,' he beamed, brushing ash from his baggy cardigan. He stubbed out the cigarette and waved the smoke away. 'Wretched health and safety... Now, what can I do for you?'

'Hello. We're looking for jewellery,' said Jamila. 'Cheap, but nice.'

'All my stuff is cheap and nice,' chuckled Bert. He took down a tray of rings and placed it on the counter. 'Have a look at that lot. All old. Old is best. Like me,' he added, with another chuckle.

Mallie and Jamila pored over the display.

'What do you think?' Jamila asked eventually.

Mallie grimaced.

'They look... *old*,' she whispered.

'That's what the man said,' hissed Jamila. 'Mal, we are in an antique shop – or hadn't you noticed?'

'Yes, yes, I know. But...'

'Perhaps a bracelet,' said Bert helpfully. 'Let me just take these out of the way.'

As he put the tray of rings back, Jamila nudged

Mallie. 'Don't look so miserable. Something will flash out at you, you'll see.'

Mallie nodded doubtfully.

'These might be more to your liking, ladies,' said Bert, as he put a tray of bracelets before them. 'Some of them are over a hundred years old.'

*Dead people's stuff*, thought Mallie. *I'm about to buy dead people's stuff for my mum to wear.* She looked around desperately to see how she could get away without hurting the old man's feelings.

'These look nice,' Jamila was saying. 'Mallie! You're not looking.'

But something else had caught Mallie's eye.

'That picture,' she said excitedly, pointing to a small, framed drawing high up on the wall. 'Could I see that?'

'A picture?' said Jamila. 'Your mum can't wear a *picture*, Mal!'

Mallie didn't reply. Her eyes were on the picture, as Bert stood on a chair and eased it off the wall. He dusted it with his sleeve and looked at the back of the frame.

'Needs a bit of cleaning,' he observed, peering short-sightedly. 'Here, have a look. I can't tell whether it's a drawing or a print, to be honest.'

Mallie took the picture. She was nodding her head and smiling.

'What?' asked Jamila. 'What's so special about that dusty old thing?'

'It's not dusty,' said Mallie. 'It's beautiful – a brilliant drawing. I know Mum would like this. It's original, I know it is – we have enough real drawings at home. But we don't have any *framed* original art – except for Mum's, of course, and that doesn't count because it's free.'

Mallie looked at the bracelet Jamila was holding up for her, and looked again at the picture.

'An old picture, or a classy bit of antique jewellery – will you make up your mind, Mallie?'

'No, listen,' went on Mallie, running her finger over the dusty glass. It was a pencil drawing of a young girl holding a rabbit. A white farmhouse with a porch stood in the background. 'There's something about this picture, Mal. It's sort of like Mum's old style, the way she used to draw. I think I'll settle for this.'

'Oh, come on, Mallie,' said Jamila. 'There are millions of pictures of sweetie-pie kids with rabbits. In those days, they had nothing better to do than stand around having their pictures done with livestock.'

'How much for this?' Mallie asked.

Bert took it from her and looked at the front, then at the back. 'No signature,' he said. 'But there's something written on this old label. Can you read it?' He handed the picture back to Mallie.

Mallie and Jamila tried to make sense of the faded brown words written in childish handwriting.

'*Mrs H,*' read Mallie. 'Hard to make it out. *Mrs H's picture*, it says. Have you ever heard of an artist called Mrs H?'

Bert shook his head.

'How come you don't know?' asked Jamila. 'I'd have thought an antique dealer would know everything about the stuff in his shop.'

Bert's belly wobbled as he chuckled. 'Dear girl,' he said, 'I buy job lots at auction. Some of it is good and some is junk. I take me chance and hope for a bit of profit.'

'Is this junk, then?' went on Jamila, nodding at the picture Mallie was holding.

'Jamila,' said Mallie. 'It isn't junk. Can't you see – it's beautiful.'

'Just trying to get the price down,' whispered Jamila.

'Well, it has no signature,' said Bert. 'So, I suppose

it's more bric á brac than antique.' He peered closer and looked up at Mallie, his eyes half-closed. 'You know, the girl looks a bit like you,' he said.

'Ha, nice one,' laughed Jamila. 'You're a flatterer!'

Bert smiled, and nodded to Mallie. 'In which case, I'll let you have it for… say…'

Mallie held her breath. She knew she wanted that picture more than anything else.

'Let's say a tenner, eh?'

'Done,' said Mallie.

# CHAPTER SIX

## LONDON, 1939

'Come away from that window,' said Tony's father. 'It's none of our business what goes on outside on a Saturday night.'

'It's the police,' said Tony, leaning on the window ledge and peering into the lamplit street at the pub opposite. 'They're pushing a gang of men inside their van. Listen, Da, they're singing.'

'The police are singing?' said his father. 'Well now, isn't that something!'

'No, Da. The men are singing.'

Tony was familiar with many of those Saturday night songs by now. When he had first arrived, he used to lie awake at night listening to songs and shouting. He'd hide his head under the blanket and tremble with fear. Would those shouting people break in here and beat him up, just as the boys in his new school had done when they jeered at his accent and the boots his father had bought him in a second-hand shop? Now it was different. He was used to the sounds of London. He was part of the fabric of the city.

'Always the same songs,' said Tony, leaning out further to get a better view. 'And they always end up in fights. Why is that, Da? It's stupid. Songs should make people happy.'

'Ex-pats,' his father explained. 'Scottish, Welsh, Irish. More and more people like us come to London for work and sing songs about their old country when they have a few beers inside them.'

'So, why the fighting?'

'Frustration, I suppose,' said his father. 'They all had to leave their homelands to find work here. And when they start to feel soppy and sentimental – even angry – after drinking, they get fired up with patriotism and work out their frustration in a fight. Then the police drive up in their Black Maria, and shunt them away to cool off in a cell. Same old story every week. The saddest songs,' he added, 'are the ones sung by the Irish.'

'Why?'

His father turned the page of his newspaper and snorted. 'Because all our wars are merry and all our songs are sad,' he said.

'What?'

'Oh, just something a writer once said about us Irish,' replied Tony's father.

'And what about you?' asked Tony. 'Do you get angry and frustrated?'

His father was silent for a moment. Then he shook his head. 'What's the point?' he said. 'I have work. That's why I came here. I just get on with it. Still...' he paused.

'Still what?'

'Still, I hanker after the old place. Old friends, familiar accents. A small town with a whole life wrapped up in it. It doesn't pass easily from the memory.'

'That doesn't make sense,' laughed Tony.

His father gave a wry smile. 'No, son, I suppose not. But inside my head it fills a great big space. Now, hadn't you better be getting to bed?'

Tony watched the Black Maria drive up the

street and listened for a while to the crowd outside The Crown. Then he closed the window. Now he was ten, he had a foldaway bed beside the wardrobe. His father had erected a clothesline between the two beds which also acted as a screen. Tony proudly boasted to his schoolmates at Saint Agnes' School that he had his own room. Since he had developed an English accent, he wasn't jeered at so much. In fact, he joined other kids in jeering at newcomers who arrived in London with strange accents. And now that he ran errands for the other tenants of Waterloo House, he had a bit of money. Mr Cooper from Number 8 was his best customer. He backed horses, which meant a daily run to the bookie's office for Tony, and whenever Mr Cooper's horse won, there was always sixpence extra for Tony to buy sweets from Mrs Matheson's sweet shop, and the odd comic. Sometimes he spent it all on giant blocks of Aero chocolate, and sometimes he made the money last longer by buying penny Buzz bars or Walls' tuppenny ice creams.

He took the Dandy comic from under his shirt, a treat from Doris for running her errands – he'd never take money from Doris – Da said not to. Then he washed in cold water and carbolic soap at the cracked sink and went into what he called his 'room'. Climbing under the blanket and an old overcoat which acted as a bedspread, he tumbled his animals out of the empty cocoa tin and arranged them in the valley between his knees for their nightly adventures in the mountainy places and dangerous jungles of worn-out, dark green tweed.

"Night, Gussie Robin, Mrs Fussyfeathers, Willie Mouse, Piglet, Granny Owl,' he would whisper to each in turn, as he put them back into their tin. But the one that stayed by his bed was his favourite, Whiskers Rabbit. The little metal models, free gifts with Bournville cocoa, had been his father's way of trying to make up for the small boy's disappointment at finding no garden or rabbit hutch when he'd arrived years ago.

'We'll collect the whole set,' his father had said. 'And they don't even need feeding.'

Tony knew that there had been times, before his father got a decent job in the garage at Kilburn Lane, when he had sacrificed his Woodbine cigarettes to buy Bournville cocoa, just to collect the animals. And sometimes, when Tony complained about living in such a grey place, he'd shout at the boy that he was doing his best. Now on Thursday nights his father went to The Crown with his workmates. When he was younger, Tony had been sent to stay with Doris at Number 14. But now Doris went to the pub too.

'It's nice and quiet before the weekend,' she said. 'And if you have a problem, ducks, you lean out the window and shout.'

It was Doris who looked after him. When he came home from school each day, she took him in until his father came home.

'You just sit quietly and amuse yourself,' she said in her husky smoker's voice, the first day she took him in. She'd put his mind at ease about the turban.

'Do I look like a princess?' she'd laughed. 'I've been called many things, sweetheart, but a princess related to a killer prince? That's a hoot! Still, if you want to call me "Your Majesty" and bow and scrape to me, I won't object.'

Doris was a dressmaker. Her room was full of half-made dresses and strips of fabric. Tony often wondered how she could find her bed at night under all that material. However, after a slow beginning he had settled into the routine of Doris's place.

It was she who taught him how to fit in by losing his accent and by not referring to his father as 'Daddy'.

'It's *Da* around these parts,' she'd said.

Thanks to her, Tony made friends with some of the boys on the street and learnt to play cricket in the alley behind the tenement. That, however, touched a raw nerve in his father.

'Foreign games,' he muttered. 'If we were at home, you'd be a hurler. I used to be a great hurler – that's our national game. All the great Irish warriors, like Finn McCool, played hurling.'

'We *are* at home, Da,' said Tony. 'You told me so when you first brought me here. Anyway, I've never even heard of hurling.'

The man sighed, and kicked at a log in the fire. The shower of sparks lit up his gaunt face.

'And you've got the accent to prove it,' he said. 'Just remember that you're Irish when you're speaking your cockney English.'

Tony always felt confused when his father talked like that. Speaking with the same accent as the other boys was what made him belong.

*But I'm not Irish or English or anything*, thought Tony. *I'm just me*. Doris had told him he was special and that it didn't matter where he came from. Ireland had become a distant place where his mother used to be and he didn't like to think of it any more, because those memories just got mixed together in a confused fog.

The noise outside became muffled and gradually died away. The only sound now was the droning voice on the wireless that his father had proudly rented from Radio Rentals since he'd got his first pay packet from the garage. Sometimes Doris came to listen, and she and his father would sing along to the music. Those were the few occasions when his father's face lifted into happiness. Recently, however, other neighbours had begun to arrive at night to listen to the radio. Not music, but just dreary, droning talk. Afterwards they sat talking in hushed tones. Tony wished it were just Doris and his father. Those were cosy times. He didn't like the voices talking in serious tones.

Then, one evening, the neighbours' faces looked shocked. An important man on the wireless had declared, 'This country is at war with Germany.'

# CHAPTER
# SEVEN

'It's lovely, Mallie,' said Sarah. She had splashed out on a Chinese takeaway and an oozy cream cake from the delicatessen for her birthday. She turned down the jazz trumpet solo on the CD player. 'Very pretty. It really is.'

'It's original.' said Mallie. 'Not a print.'

'I know,' said her mum. 'Superb little drawing. Lovely detail. Look at the fine line shading.'

'The what?'

'Shading with lines,' replied Sarah. 'My mother showed me how to do it when I was little...' She broke off and stared at the floor.

'Oh, Mum,' said Mallie. Any mention of Gran was still upsetting. Though sometimes, when she felt the need, Sarah would talk to Mallie about her mother. There had been just the two of them, Gran and Sarah. Gran had doted on her daughter, giving her the best education possible. 'No clawing your way up the ladder like I had to,' she'd tell her.

Gran was an artist. She had left for America when Sarah graduated from Art College.

'You're on your way now, love,' she'd said. 'No point in the two of us competing against one another here. And I've always wanted to see the world.'

She did well in America with her illustrations for books, calendars and greeting cards, earning enough to fly home to England for holidays. Then she decided to return to England for good, and Mallie had happy memories of Gran fussing over her, spoiling her and taking her for long, chatty walks and showing her how to draw ducks. Then, just four months later, Mallie's dad was driving Gran back to her new apartment after Sarah's birthday party when the car skidded into a wall. Gran was killed instantly. Dad died two days later.

Neither Mallie nor her mum cared to dwell on

that bad time. Sarah packed most of their belongings into the attic. Even now, Mallie avoided looking up at the attic door because of the memories it brought back. She wanted to remember Dad and Gran as they'd been, not as the dead owners of stored stuff.

'You could do that, Mum,' said Mallie.

'Do what?'

'You could do pictures like that. You used to do brilliant drawings of real things before... before...'

'Before my style went big and bold?' Sarah forced a laugh.

'Well, you should try this style again. It might sell.'

'Hanging on walls in junk shops, Mallie? I don't think so. Oops,' she added, when she saw Mallie's face. 'I didn't mean... But you can't have had much money to buy it. Oh, sorry, Mal. I love it. I really do, and I'll treasure it always. You know me, I don't put a price on things. It's the thought...'

'Oh, forget it, Mum. Stop digging a hole to bury yourself in. I'm just saying, it's the sort of thing that you're good at. *Were* good at. That's what attracted me to this picture.'

'Look, love,' said Sarah, pushing aside the piles of bills on the mantelpiece. 'I'm putting it here, in pride of place, see? And I really love it, Mallie.' Then she frowned, and peered more closely at the picture.

'What?' asked Mallie. 'If you're looking for a signature, there isn't one. But it *is* original, like I've said.'

'Yes,' replied Sarah. 'I know it's original. It's just...' Then she shook her head and laughed. 'There's something about it,' she said, half to herself.

'Oh, come off it, Mum,' laughed Mallie. 'No need to go overboard. All the drama you can muster won't cancel out what you said about junk shops.'

🐇🐇🐇

'Did she like it, Mallie?' Jamila asked next day, as the girls met at their usual corner on the way to school.

'She did,' said Mallie. 'She liked it.'

'She didn't, did she? I know by your face. If she really liked it, you'd say she loved it to bits.'

'Oh, give me a break,' said Mallie, kicking a discarded Coke tin.

'Ah, I was right,' laughed Jamila. 'You should have taken my advice and bought a bracelet. Hey, Mal, what's wrong?' She stopped, and put her hand on

Mallie's shoulder. 'I'm sorry if I've...'

Mallie wrinkled her nose to fight back tears. 'I thought I could get Mum back to doing what she does best. I just hate to see her taking on crummy job after crummy job. She makes a joke of it every time she gets the push, but I know she's burning up inside. Dragging herself down to the job centre will do her head in. She'll sink into misery. She always does. I can't bear all that. Not any more.'

'She'll get another job,' said Jamila.

'Maybe. But for how long?

'Oh, Mallie,' said Jamila. 'Don't think like that. She's a bright old bird, your mum. She'll get by.'

'That's just it, Jam. "Getting by" is a bore.'

'Well,' Jamila said. 'At least you have your part-time job, so you don't have to sting your ma for money.'

'That's the ironic bit,' snorted Mallie. 'I have good pocket money, but I can't tell her because she'd blow a fuse. So she still struggles to give me money, but I know the money from my father and granny has dwindled. See? Now I even feel guilty for telling you.'

'Look, guilt won't get you anywhere except to a care home,' said Jamila. 'Things will work out.

You get working on Steve...'

'Press *Delete* there, Jam,' Mallie laughed, in spite of herself. 'You dizzy ditz. Give it a rest. It's not going to happen.'

'Don't knock romance, Mallie. It's what makes the world go round.'

'Oh, listen to yourself,' laughed Mallie. 'For a tough old boot, you sure talk mushy rubbish. Come on, we'll be late.'

# CHAPTER EIGHT

Later that day, while she was grooming a Yorkshire terrier, Mallie recalled Jamila's words. She glanced over at Steve. *Nice build,* she thought. *Handsome, in a rugged, oldie sort of way. Intelligent, fun, solid and dependable. He'd do for Mum. Maybe Jamila, with her romantic notions, has a point.*

Steve looked up and caught her staring.

'Yes, Mallie?' he said.

Mallie blinked. 'Nothing, Steve,' she said, brushing the dog briskly to hide her embarrassment. *Just wondering how I'd get you to meet my mum,* she thought.

This was to happen sooner than Mallie expected.

Because she was small and slight, it was Mallie's job to set up the small-animal boxes in the window, setting the window shade to the right length to keep out the sunlight. On that particular Saturday, she was settling a couple of hamsters into their cage, when she heard a rap on the window.

'Mum!'

And Mum it was. Mum with a face like thunder. She stormed into the shop, her calf-length, multi-coloured cardigan billowing.

'Explain,' she said.

'I have a part-time job,' said Mallie.

'You what? Haven't we talked about this?' said Sarah. 'And what did I say? I said *no way*. What part of *no way* do you not understand, Mallie? Time enough for work when you leave school.'

'Oh, Mum. What harm is there? I love this job – it's only a few hours a week. I'd have told you...'

'Like when?' said Sarah. 'I don't like you being sneaky, Mal.'

'Mum! I wasn't being sneaky. That's a rotten word.'

'So why couldn't you have talked this over with me before you took it on yourself to skivvy in a pet shop?'

'Because I knew you'd react exactly as you're doing now,' retorted Mallie. 'I'm making my own pocket money, Mum. So you don't have to worry about giving me money. How do you think I feel, taking money from you when I know you can't afford it? Where's the harm in having a job I like? I can go to the High Street and buy clothes and things, instead of standing by, totally miserable, watching my mates top up on trendy stuff. And it doesn't interfere with school, believe me.'

Sarah was shaking her head. 'I make enough for both of us,' she said. 'Sometimes it's a bit thin, but we manage.'

'Mum! There's no point in buttering your pride. I'm fed up with managing. I'm bored with your moods. I'm sorry, but it's true. You go hyper when you get a new job, then it falls apart and you mooch about like a martyr. If Gran were here, she'd tell you…'

'Leave Gran out of this. You hardly remember her.'

'Is there something wrong?'

Mallie and her mum turned.

'It's all right, Steve,' muttered Mallie. 'This… woman is just leaving.'

'Leaving?' said Sarah, frowning at her daughter.

'Don't dismiss me like that, young lady. As for you,' she turned to Steve again, 'taking on an underage child without parental consent – you should be ashamed.'

It was Steve's turn to frown. He looked questioningly at Mallie. Mallie sighed. Why wasn't Jamila here to back her up?

'I thought you had discussed this with your parents, Mallie,' he said.

'I know. I'm sorry,' said Mallie. 'But, you see' – she nodded towards her mother – 'I knew this would happen. And I wanted the job, I really did.'

'She only works a few hours each week, you know,' said Steve to Sarah. 'She's a bright girl, and you can rest assured she doesn't neglect her studies. I really appreciate her help.'

'I'm sure,' muttered Sarah.

'Mum, Steve pays me very well, and I love the work. Please stop making a fuss. You're just embarrassing me.'

'I think you should come home,' said Sarah.

'No,' insisted Mallie. 'Unlike you, Mum, I'm holding on to my job. Get used to it.'

'Hold on a sec,' put in Steve. 'Let's not get over-excited.'

He turned to Sarah. 'I'm sorry you feel like this,' he said firmly. 'But if it bothers you to have Mallie earning a few hours' money, then there's really nothing more to be said. You are her mother, after all.'

'But...' began Mallie. Steve put his hand out to silence her.

'The most reasonable thing would be to let Mallie work for, say, two more weeks,' he said calmly. 'That way, I'll be able to advertise for a new part-timer, and Mallie at least has the dignity of finishing properly.'

Sarah softened. 'Fair enough, I suppose,' she said. 'But don't think I'm not annoyed,' she added.

'And you have every right to be,' agreed Steve. 'My name is Steve Armstrong, by the way,' he added. He held out his hand. 'I'm holding the fort here for my father. He's in a convalescent home for a while.'

Mallie marvelled at his diplomacy. Sarah took his hand. Still, being Mum, she had to have the parting shot.

'We'll talk about this later, Mallie,' she said.

'I'll bet,' muttered Mallie, as her mother opened the shop door.

'You handled that very well,' she said to Steve,

when the door closed behind her mother. 'I'm really sorry about all this.'

'And so you should be,' said Steve. 'You've deceived both your mother and me, you know. You gave me to understand that your parents approved. I hope your father isn't going to arrive next and challenge me to a duel, Mallie. Lasers at dawn. Anyway, always be upfront. Now, could we get that window finished?'

🐰🐰🐰

'I felt like a dork,' Mallie said to Jamila later on her mobile, as she recounted the confrontation. 'Can you imagine? Mum made a show of me. I wanted to lie down and die. I'll never forgive her. Never.'

'Yes, you will,' laughed Jamila. 'He's dead cool, is Steve.'

'He was great. Except he was a bit miffed with me for pretending that my "parents" were OK about the job.'

'How's your mum now?' asked Jamila.

'Don't know,' replied Mallie. 'We haven't spoken. I took supper up to my room and I haven't been downstairs since. Let her stew. I hope her next job, if she gets one, will have long hours. Very long hours.'

Jamila laughed. 'You don't mean that,' she said.

'Don't I? Ask your dad if he has any relations in India who'd take on a pain in the butt like my mother. Preferably a job like... like mucking out elephant stables. Or knitting carpets.'

The following Wednesday, Mallie felt a bit sheepish meeting Steve again. But she needn't have worried. He was his usual cheery self, and the hours passed as normal. At the end of the day, he was the one to look sheepish.

'I have a favour to ask, Mallie,' he said.

What? Mallie bit her lip. Did he want her to leave now?

'It's a rabbit that's a bit poorly,' Steve went on. 'I'm going to collect my father this evening, but he can't be left on his own – the rabbit, I mean. I've had his cage beside my bed for the past two nights. He seems to be doing OK, but he needs watching. Do you think you could take him home with you? It's just for tonight.'

Mallie let out a sigh of relief. Not only was she not being dismissed, but she was being given responsibility.

'No problem,' she said. 'I'll watch him every second of the time.'

'You needn't go that far,' laughed Steve. 'Just cast the odd glance in his direction, that's all. Don't worry,' he added, 'he won't croak on you. Like I said, he's on the mend. Just make sure he has plenty of water, and I'll give you some tablets to give him last thing tonight. I'm really grateful.'

It was only on her way home that Mallie wondered how her mother would react to the overnight lodger. She went through both sides of the argument in her mind. By the time she turned the key in the front door, she had an entire collection of angry responses in her head to fire at her mother's objections.

'Before you ask, Mum,' she said defensively, 'it's a sick rabbit and I'm minding him for tonight. He'll be in my room while I'm doing my homework, and you won't have to look at him, so don't worry.'

'Fine by me,' said Sarah, stooping to look at the rabbit. 'Poor thing. Is he very bad?'

Mallie was taken aback. Why couldn't her mum be predictable? 'He'll be all right,' she muttered. She headed upstairs with the cage.

'Don't you want some supper, Mal?'

'It's OK. I bought some stuff at the deli,'

Mallie replied. 'Paid for with my own money which I earned doing work I like.'

'Oh Mal, I'm sorry. I acted like a… a mad thing. Just the thought of you needing to find work – it made me feel guilty and useless. You're a good girl, Mal. I wish I could give you more.'

'Forget it, Mum,' muttered Mallie from the stairs. 'It's OK.'

# CHAPTER NINE
# WARTIME LONDON

'Don't dawdle, Tony,' said Doris, pulling the boy along. 'No point in staring. Let's go back home.'

Tony reluctantly turned away from the people huddled around what was once a terrace of houses. Three of the houses, reduced to rubble, left a gap like the mouth of a giant who'd had several teeth knocked out. Ash was everywhere – now and then little wisps of it rose and gusted in the breeze. Small fires still spluttered and sparked under the débris. He should be used to the bombing by now, but Doris said you never get used to living on the edge of death.

'You just don't know where hell's gates are going to be opened up again by those Nazis,' she said.

A gable wall stood as a stark reminder of the family which had once lived in the house Tony and Doris were now passing. Tattered wallpaper hung from the single standing wall. An iron fireplace still had the remains of a fire in the grate. An armchair with a flowery covering lay upturned, its springs stuck out like the antennae of a disabled monster. Smouldering beams and piles of bricks were all that was left of most of the other houses. Men with tin hats were searching through the rubble.

'Where are the people?' Tony asked Doris.

'I don't know,' she replied without changing her pace, as she picked her way through a jigsaw of masonry. 'I couldn't bring myself to ask. Just keep your head down, Tony. We'll survive. And make sure you always have that gas mask with you.'

Tony clutched the gas mask he carried everywhere, and tried to keep up.

'Potatoes,' Doris was saying. 'I'm told there are potatoes in the market near the church. If we can get potatoes and eggs, Tony, we'll dine like kings.'

*Potatoes and eggs.* For a brief moment Tony thought of Mrs Mooney. But now he couldn't even remember what she looked like.

It didn't seem strange that Doris now ate with him and his father. She was good at cooking things in one saucepan. The Ministry of Aircraft Production had urged everyone to hand in anything made from aluminium to help the war effort.

At first, Tony's father protested.

'It's not my war,' he'd said. 'My country is neutral.'

But Doris put him right. 'It bloody *is* your war, chuck,' she said. 'You're over here taking the King's shilling, so you'll bloody well do what we're all doing. You'll fall in with everyone else who's trying to give Hitler a kick up the bum. I've already handed over my precious thimbles for the war effort – and me a dressmaker!'

The war made people pull together. When Mrs Carter's son was reported missing in action, all the tenants in Waterloo House called to see her, bringing food and soft words. And when old Mr Jessop in Number 5 and Jack Thompson, the plumber at Number 3, joined the Home Guard, they were the pride of everyone at Waterloo House. At school, many of the children talked about going to an underground station for shelter during the air raids. Tony wanted his father to take him down too. The boys said it was fun, even though they had to walk a long way to get there. But when the dreaded siren sounded, Tony, his father and Doris took blankets down to the squashy space in the basement. It was cold and bleak there, but somehow Tony felt secure, tucked up between his father and Doris among the residents of Waterloo House, and people in the street whose houses had no basements.

'Can't stand crowded places, me,' said Mrs Carter, as she heaved her big body into the farthest corner. 'Push over there, and give me room to breathe.' But she always brought her homemade biscuits to share.

And so they'd sit listening to the dull thuds, and they'd wonder aloud which part of the city had been hit. Every explosion sent a shiver through Tony's skinny body. First there was a distant whistling sound that made everyone freeze, followed by that dull thud. Same pattern every night. Sometimes the thuds came frighteningly close, then receded.

'Missed again,' Mr Cooper would say, with a nervous laugh. 'Passed right by us.'

'This time round,' someone else would add.

'You're safe, lad,' Doris would whisper in Tony's ear. 'See? They've gone past us.'

But Tony knew she was as scared as he was.

Some of his classmates had Anderson shelters in their back gardens. Tony wished they could have one too, because they sounded so cosy, packed with food and comfy bedding and lights to read by so that you could take your mind off the terrifying noise. But there was no garden at the back of this house, so he'd have to make do with the basement, clutching his cocoa tin full of animals.

Then there was that awful anticipation when the all-clear sounded and they emerged from the shelter. Whose house would not be there? At times like this, Tony would grip his father's hand. A big, safe hand.

One night Mr Hafner, who ran a butcher's shop across the road, didn't turn up when the siren went.

'He was taken away,' said Mr Cooper.

'Taken away where?' asked Tony. He liked Mr Hafner, who talked funny and sometimes gave him leftover sausages at the end of the day.

'They're rounding up Germans,' said Tony's father. 'Same thing in the garage where I work. Two of the lads were taken away last week.'

'Why?' asked Tony.

'They're German, ' said his father, 'and the Government aren't taking any chances. They're putting German people who have settled here into camps. It's just for the duration of the war. They'll be back soon.'

'Camps?' queried Tony.

'Prisons, more like,' Mrs Carter's voice came from her corner. 'They're afraid they might be spies.'

'That's not fair,' objected Tony. 'Mr Hafner isn't a spy. He's just the butcher.'

'Aye. And that Hitler is a butcher too,' snorted Mrs Carter.

'Not the same,' Doris whispered to Tony.

'I still don't understand, Doris.'

'Huh, what's there to understand about war?' she sighed.

On Sundays, Doris insisted that Tony and his father come with her to the park. 'No point in being stuck here waiting for the next bomb to drop,' she said, as she drew lines up the backs of her legs to look like stocking seams. 'A trip to the park will keep us sane. Bit of fresh air.'

But often the air was anything but fresh as they passed more and more bombed buildings on the way. Everywhere seemed to be covered in dreary grey ash, and the smoky smell stayed on their clothes long after they got home.

'It's like Pompeii,' Tony's father said once, as they passed a wrecked warehouse that was still smouldering.

'What's Pompeii?' asked Tony.

'Just what I was going to ask,' said Doris. 'Your da and his books!'

Tony's father laughed. He liked it when Doris referred to his love of books with a certain pride in her voice. He could now afford to indulge in the new Penguin sixpenny paperbacks, which opened up the whole world of literature to people like him with little money to spare.

'Pompeii was a city in Italy,' he explained. 'It was swallowed up in lava when a volcano called Vesuvius erupted. Everything was turned to ashes.'

'And did people die then, too?' said Tony.

'Just as they do now,' his father nodded. 'Except that now it's not a natural disaster.'

'What do you mean?' asked Tony.

'He means that that Nazi lunatic over there is doing all this on purpose,' put in Doris angrily.

'Why don't we bomb him back?' went on Tony.

'We do,' said Doris. 'Our lads are giving as good as this to the Germans.'

'So are there German people sheltering from our

bombs? People just like us?'

Doris shrugged, and looked at Tony's father.

'There are,' he said. 'Ordinary people like us. That's war for you.'

'It's stupid,' said Tony. 'And it's not very merry, is it?'

'Merry?' asked Doris. 'Where are you getting that from?'

'Da once told me that all our wars are merry and all our songs are sad,' replied the boy.

Tony's father shook his head and smiled. 'A writer said that,' he said. 'George Bernard Shaw. But he said it about Ireland.'

'Maybe we should have stayed in Ireland,' went on Tony. 'A merry war would be better than this one.'

Everywhere they went, people with strained faces seemed eager to greet them. Coming from Ireland, where he could remember the friendship of a whole town, Tony had had to grow used to Londoners keeping themselves private. Now, in spite of bombs and fires and rubble, Londoners were suddenly friendly.

'Good afternoon,' someone said, as they passed a group sweeping up broken glass outside a recently bombed building.

'Good to see the sunshine,' added someone else.

'Hello,' said Doris. 'Anyone... hurt?' Tony looked up at her. Doris usually didn't ask, in case the answer was bad. Perhaps this war was changing her too. He didn't want her to change. He wanted her to stay soft. A soft-centred nut, his father called her.

'No. Everyone was down in the shelter, thank goodness.'

As usual, Tony's father said nothing, but nodded in sympathy.

'It's because of his Irish accent,' Doris told the boy later, when he asked her why his father didn't talk to the people they passed. 'He feels he's not part of all the camaraderie that's grown out of the war. He thinks that if he opens his mouth, people will turn on him for not being British. Silly beggar. I've told him so many times. But will he listen? Stubborn old mule, your da.'

Back on the street, games of cricket had been replaced by bomb-site exploration. With a small gang of boys, Tony spent his days after school trawling the neighbourhood for bombed areas. Some of the older bomb-sites were ideal for playing cowboys. You soon forgot about the smell of ashes as you charged with the cavalry against the baddies. They took it in turns to play baddies. And Tony felt really proud one day when one of the older boys smeared a moustache on his face with a cold cinder, when it was his turn to be bad. That evening, several tired and filthy little moustachioed Hitler cowboys went home.

'Look at the state of you,' Doris said, as she pulled Tony's shirt off and scrubbed his face. 'If your da knew what you were up to, he'd leather you – and give me a load of grief for letting you off,' she added.

'I'll say nothing if you say nothing,' Tony said, and grinned. It was easy to get around Doris.

One afternoon, Tony waited for the boys in the usual place. Only two turned up. Peter and George.

'Where are the others?' he asked.

'Evacuated,' said Peter. 'All the children at their school were evacuated.'

'Do you... does that mean they're dead?' Tony asked.

'No,' replied George. 'They've been taken on a train to the country.'

'Why?'

Peter shrugged. 'Some government thing,' he said. 'They're rounding up children like us and sending us to stay with people down in the country to be away from the bombing.'

'All the children like us?' asked Tony.

'I think so,' put in George. 'We're being sent next week, me and Peter. Miss at our school said so.'

'Well, you won't get me doing that,' Tony said. 'I'm staying here, I am.'

'If you're told to go, you'll have to,' said George, 'if your school gets picked.'

'I'll hide,' said Tony.

'Ha!' laughed George. 'They'll find you, and send you so far away that you'll never get back.'

Tony tried to put the thought from his mind, but visions of separation haunted him.

'You look a bit miserable,' Doris said to him as he let himself in, dragging his feet. Tony said nothing. He threw his schoolbag into a corner and sat on a bundle of clothes left with Doris for repairs and renovation – few people could afford to buy new clothes these days. He watched the rhythmic movement of Doris's feet working the treadle of the sewing machine, wisps of cigarette smoke wafting up to the high, peeling ceiling. Doris glanced over at him as she turned a shabby grey coat inside out. 'Well? Am I to be privileged to hear what's eating you, or will we keep a wall of silence between us?'

Tony sighed, and rested his chin on his hands.

'They're sending children away,' he said. 'Peter and George's school are going next week.'

Doris bit at a thread with her teeth.

'I said they're...'

'I know what you said,' put in Doris. 'I know.'

'You know?'

Doris sighed and nodded.

'I won't go,' said Tony. 'I wouldn't leave you and me da. Not me.'

Doris put down the coat and turned towards the boy. Tony frowned. He knew there was something serious coming.

'It's for the best, ducks,' she said gently. 'It's to keep you all safe.'

Tony pulled away. 'But I'd never go,' he said again. 'This is my home. I won't go to no stinking countryside.'

Later that night, when another air raid siren sent them to the basement, Tony's father explained the move to the boy, as the bombs blasted one after another around the city.

'It's a good thing,' he said, his arm around Tony. 'You're going next week. You'll be with lots of other children and you'll have great fun. Like a holiday,

Tony. That's a much nicer word than "evacuated", isn't it? And you'll have none of this,' he added, as the terrifying pre-thud whistle of a bomb screeched somewhere above them.

Tony felt a dread that started in his chest and clawed its way up into his mind – a sickeningly familiar dread that he'd last felt when he was five.

# CHAPTER TEN

Mallie was vaguely conscious of her bedroom door opening during the night. Just Mum checking. She'd been doing that every night for as far back as Mallie could remember. *Time she gave it up,* thought Mallie. *Or maybe she's checking to see that I haven't climbed out of my window to take a job in a night club, now that she's got me sacked from the day-job.*

She drifted back to sleep.

Her mum had left next morning by the time Mallie and the rabbit came downstairs. Another interview, maybe?

Mallie yawned and put the rabbit cage on the table.

'Are you still alive then, Bun?' she asked. The rabbit was lively and seemed to be hungry. He was gnawing at a chunk of carrot.

Mallie peered closer. There had been no carrot there last night. *He must have been sitting on it*, she mused. But when she looked at the sink, she saw carrot scrapings on the draining-board. Mum...

'Don't eat that, Bunny,' she said. 'I bet it's laced with strychnine.' What was Mum doing, taking the rabbit from Mallie's room to feed it, and then sneaking it back again?

She found out when she sat down at the table. Propped up against the milk jug was an exquisite drawing of the rabbit, complete with fine shading.

*Do you forgive your old mum?'* was the message scrawled underneath the drawing.

Mallie laughed out loud. 'You old fraud, Mum.' She looked more closely at the drawing, marvelling at the detail of the rabbit's fur and the gentle highlights around the ears. Suddenly her world seemed a brighter place. She picked up the birthday present from the mantelpiece in the living-room and compared the two drawings. Magic!

*I knew you could do it, Mum*, she thought. *I knew there was magic in this picture the moment I spotted it.*

*I was drawn to it.* She laughed at her own pun as she put the sketch between the pages of her French homework to show Jamila.

Much as she liked looking after the rabbit, she was glad to be returning it to Steve later.

'Don't go having a heart attack, Bunny,' she warned, as she put the framed picture on the kitchen dresser.

🐰🐰🐰

Jamila was waiting at her usual place. 'What's that?' she asked. 'A rabbit?'

'No,' replied Mallie. 'It's not a rabbit. It's Mum. I did some seriously damaging voodoo last night and, hey presto, a docile mum with big ears.'

'You're in a cheerful mood,' said Jamila, 'for someone who was scraping the bottom of the emotional barrel yesterday.'

'I think Mum might be coming round.' Mallie stopped, and took the sketch from her schoolbag. 'Look at this,' she said.

'Wow!' Jamila responded just the way Mallie had hoped. 'Mega. Your mum did this?'

Mallie nodded.

'You should show this to Steve,' went on Jamila. 'He'd be dead chuffed.'

'You think?' said Mallie, putting the picture back into her homework copy.

'Yeah. That would wipe out your mum's daft behaviour last week and show him that she's not totally mental. You still want him and her to click, don't you?'

Mallie shrugged. 'Not sure,' she said. 'I don't think it would work. Best just to…'

'Oh, don't be such a wuss,' scoffed Jamila. 'He'd keep her in line.'

'Well, maybe,' said Mallie. 'Not now, though. I'll leave Bunny with Jim, the school caretaker, until home-time. Maybe then I'll show the sketch to Steve.'

But Steve was in a rush when Mallie arrived at the pet shop after school. 'Forgot to get groceries,' he said. 'I've been so used to takeaways while my father was convalescing that I didn't think to get in food. Can you manage for half an hour, Mallie?'

'No problem,' replied Mallie. After all, the more indispensable she proved to be, the better – especially if Mum was softening. Apart from a dribble of customers buying bird seed and cat litter, the shop was quiet. She checked on her overnight lodger and was pleased to see him nibbling his food. This reminded her of the sketch. She took it out and propped it beside the rabbit's cage.

'Not many of your lot get to have their portraits done,' she said. 'Count yourself among the privileged.'

'Are you on your own?'

Mallie looked up to see Jamila.

She nodded.

'Well,' went on Jamila, ambling over to a hamster cage. 'Now's our chance, Mallie.'

'Chance to do what?' asked Mallie.

'To release all these creatures. Give them their freedom to live lives where they can move about, go shopping, chat with hamsters from other places, shoot the breeze, chill out and have hamster raves, instead of being cooped up in sawdust and pointlessly treading those ridiculous hamster wheels. Where's the fun in that? God forbid I come back as a hamster. I think I'd slit my throat.'

'You a furry hamster?' laughed Mallie. 'Fanged tiger with attitude, more like. Anyway, they're happy, these hamsters. They don't know any other sort of life. Come to think of it, have you ever heard of a place where hamsters run wild? Vicious hamsters hunting in packs?'

'Well, let's just set them off into the street and then they'll be wild. The ones that are not flattened, that is. Look at all these lumps of fur – rabbits and hamsters – just sitting there, brain-dead. Let's shoo them all out to a life.'

'What sort of talk is that?' said a voice. 'Come away from those cages, you two.'

The girls turned to see a tall, thin man, hobbling with the aid of a walking stick, emerge from the back of the shop. Jamila looked at Mallie and raised her eyebrows. 'Steve's dad,' whispered Mallie, 'I think.'

'If you're not buying anything, then go and find somewhere else to congregate,' the man went on.

'You must be Mr Armstrong,' said Mallie. 'I'm Mallie Kelly. I'm Steve's assistant.'

'Assistant?' said Mr Armstrong, staring at Mallie's school uniform. 'And when did my son start hiring children? Go somewhere else and play your games.'

'She's not a child, she's a teenager,' said Jamila. 'And she does her job pretty well. This place would have fallen apart if it weren't for our Mallie. You should be grateful, instead of attacking...'

'It's all right, Jamila,' put in Mallie. 'She doesn't

mean that,' she went on, turning to Mr Armstrong. 'I help Steve out after school. Surely he told you?'

'Huh! He should have asked me first. Anyway, I'm back now, so you won't be needed any more, young lady. How much do we owe you?'

Mallie looked helplessly at Jamila, who shrugged and mouthed the words, 'Old fart.' Mr Armstrong was fiddling with the cash register, muttering to himself.

'What do I do now?' whispered Mallie.

Jamila frowned meaningfully. 'You stand your ground,' she whispered, 'until Steve comes back and sorts this geezer out.'

'I don't want to cause trouble,' mumbled Mallie. 'Not between Steve and his dad.'

'So, how much?' asked Mr Armstrong.

'I don't know,' began Mallie. 'My days are not up yet.'

'Well, call back tomorrow and we'll pay you off.'

'OK,' said Mallie. 'If you say so.' She picked up her schoolbag and ushered Jamila out before she could say anything.

'The old fossil,' said Jamila, when they were outside. 'It's a wonder the animals haven't all died screaming, with a dragon like him breathing on them. You should have faced him down, Mal. After all, it was Steve who hired you, not him – Mr A.P. Armstrong, it says on his card. What does A.P. stand for? Angry Prat?'

'Not worth thinking about,' muttered Mallie. 'Well, this saves me working out my notice. Mum will be pleased. Bloody adults,' she added. 'They always get their way. Come on, let's buy a couple of Magnums. My treat. We might as well spend while I still have the money.'

🐇🐇🐇

Mallie's mum was in a sombre mood when Mallie got home. What was it now? Another failed job interview? One never knew with Mum. As always, Mallie felt it was somehow her fault. Everything boiled down to the fact that Mum was having to support her. Except that this time, she hadn't the energy to try and cheer her mother up.

'I'll eat in my room, Mum,' she said. 'Piles of homework.'

Sarah nodded. 'Whatever you like, Mal,' she said. 'There's a lasagne in the fridge.'

'I'll eat it later,' said Mallie, already on her way

upstairs. She threw her schoolbag on the bed, and threw herself after it.

'*Lfs a btch.*' she texted Jamila.

'*Y?*' Jamila replied.

'*Bldy awfll!*' went on Mallie. '*Misry.*'

'*Ull gt ovr it.*'

'*Gdnite.*'

It was much later when Mallie heard the doorbell ring. Nine-thirty. Who could be calling at this hour? Probably someone asking for money. *Deal with it, Mum.*

'Mallie!' her mother called up from the hall.

*Someone for me?* thought Mallie. But when she came downstairs and saw Steve in the hall, she smelled trouble.

'Hello, Mallie. My father…' he began.

'Yes, I met him,' said Mallie. 'Don't worry. I left quietly.'

'That's why I came,' put in Steve, holding up a large envelope. 'It's this,' he said, producing the drawing of the rabbit from the envelope. 'Was it you who left it beside the rabbit's hutch?'

Mallie looked at her mum again. Sarah was frowning. 'Yes,' she said wearily. 'Mum did it. I thought you'd like to see it.'

'I did that for you, Mal,' put in Sarah.

'Yes, I know,' said Mallie. 'It's totally brilliant, Mum. That's why I took it to show Steve. Forgot to bring it home. Thanks, Steve.' She reached out for the drawing.

But Steve wasn't about to part with it.

'It's amazing,' he said.

'Thank you,' said Sarah.

'No, I really mean it,' said Steve. 'That's why I've come round – why I went to the trouble of looking up your address in the phone book. I want to talk to you.'

'About what?' said Mallie.

'You'd better come and sit down,' said Sarah, leading the way into the sitting-room and taking books and magazines off the sofa. Mallie followed, wondering what was coming next, and whether it would end in embarrassment. Steve sat on the saggy sofa, his long legs stretched out to accommodate the sinking sensation of worn-out upholstery. He cleared his throat and looked at the drawing of the rabbit.

'I have a proposition,' he said, pausing to see if there would be any reaction. Mallie and her mum waited. 'We could work together,' he went on.

'Oh, yes?' said Sarah. Mallie wanted to shake her, tell her to be excited about whatever it was Steve was offering. But Mum was being ultra-cool.

'Work together how?' asked Mallie.

'Well,' he began, 'as you know, my father sells pets. Not the most lucrative business in the world, but he's happy. A gentle livelihood after his years as a vet. He gets a bit stroppy now and then, but that's just a cover.'

*Cover for what?* Mallie wondered.

'Mr Armstrong,' said Sarah. 'Why are you telling me this?'

'Sorry,' said Steve. 'I'm rambling on a bit. Thing is,' he fiddled with his hands, suddenly seeming bashful. 'Thing is, business is slow. OK, people always want bird seed and pet food, but selling small animals gets a bit shaky when the small animals are slow to sell and suddenly become bigger animals – if you catch my drift.'

'They're harder to sell when they're older,' said Sarah.

'Exactly,' replied Steve. 'When the cuddly look goes, they lose their selling power.'

'But what's this got to do with my drawing?' asked Sarah.

'Well, I was thinking. If you drew pictures of the pets and they were on offer with the animals themselves…'

'An added attraction,' put in Sarah, with a grin.

'Exactly,' said Steve. 'Potential buyers would get a double deal – a pet plus a portrait.'

Sarah rested her chin on her hands and mulled over Steve's words.

'Oh, Mum!' exclaimed Mallie. 'What's to stop you? I think it's a brilliant idea. That drawing of the rabbit is mega. Just like…' She looked at the mantelpiece, but remembered that she had left the picture she'd bought – the inspiration for her mother's drawing – in the kitchen.

Sarah sighed. 'I only did that for you, Mallie,' she said. 'It was just a bit of fun. Anyway,' she went on, turning to Steve. 'How would this work out?'

'Ah, the business end of it,' said Steve. 'Well, I could bring small animals here for you to draw. We could offer the sketches at an agreed price – unframed.'

'And your commission?' asked Sarah.

Steve shrugged. 'I'll have had my payment. The offer only goes through with the sale of the animal.'

'Go on, Mum,' enthused Mallie. 'You could do ten

of those in a week. Think of it!'

'Let's not get ahead of ourselves, Mallie,' said Sarah, though Mallie could see from the light in her eyes that she was excited. 'Look, I'll think about it, Mr Armstrong. I'll let you know tomorrow. OK?'

'Steve,' said Steve. 'Please call me Steve.'

'Sarah,' said Mallie's mum softly. 'My name is Sarah. And I'll consider your suggestion, Steve. I really will,' she added, with a smile.

Mallie wanted to shake her mum.

'What is it with you, Mum?' she said, when Steve had left. 'You're being handed a cushy job. You should have jumped at it. You're one weird woman – do you know that?'

Her Mum laughed. 'Rule number one, Mallie,' she said. 'Never play your hand until you're sure of your cards. My mother told me that. As I said, I'll think about it.'

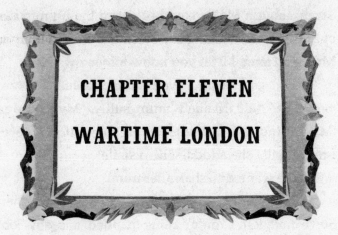

# CHAPTER ELEVEN
# WARTIME LONDON

The station was crowded with whitefaced parents and sobbing children. There was a smell of damp coats from the heavy rain. Doris gripped Tony's hand.

'Don't you go getting soft on me, lad,' she said. But Tony could see that she was the one who was getting soft. 'Just remember,' she went on, 'that this is to keep you safe. When all this stupid war lark is over, you, me and your da will be back together again. Someone's going to put a bomb under that Hitler sooner or later, then all this will be finished.'

'I don't want to go,' insisted Tony. 'Why can't I stay with you and Da? I don't want to go to some strangers, Doris. Look at all these kids. I'm older than most of them. Please let me stay with you and Da. I'll work. I'll help…'

'Tony, my treasure, we've been through all this before – you, me and your father. Look, there's Miss Gilmore, your teacher. Hello, Miss Gilmore!' she called out, as she gripped Tony's hand even tighter.

Miss Gilmore was ticking off a list.

'Tony,' she beamed. It wasn't a real smile – more a mask. She was upset. Everyone was upset. Tony tried to take a deep breath, but there wasn't much air. Other youngsters from Tony's school, each one wearing a label and carrying a suitcase and gas mask, were being ushered on board the train. Some of them were as young as four.

'I'm not a baby,' muttered Tony, trying not to cry.

'Of course not,' agreed Miss Gilmore, glancing meaningfully at Doris. 'But you bigger children can look after the younger ones. We're depending on you to do that.'

'See?' said Doris. 'You're doing the country a service.'

'I feel like a parcel,' Tony muttered sullenly, fingering the luggage label pinned to his jacket with his name and destination written on it.

'You take off that label, and I will personally come and clip your earhole,' snapped Doris. 'We need to know that you're safe, your da and me...'

'And I need to know that you're safe,' put in Tony. 'I'm scared, Doris.' He was trying hard not to let his lip quiver, but now that he was almost on board, he could feel the panic begin to crowd into his throat. 'Please, Doris...'

'Now, now,' said Doris, unclasping the boy's fingers from her hand. 'What did I say? Our chaps will have that Hitler out of the way in no time at all. Then we'll celebrate with a party. How about that, eh? A big party with—'

'Stop, Doris!' Tony sobbed. 'I don't want a party. I just want to stay with you and Da. Please. I don't want any more strange places.'

Doris's face softened as she hugged the boy. 'We'll be here when you get back,' she said. 'Your da and me, we'll be here. Just you remember that. Now go and get a seat. And you make sure that you eat those jam sandwiches.'

Miss Gilmore nodded at Doris as she ushered

the reluctant boy on board. With a last comforting squeeze of his fingers, Doris went back and joined the parents putting up a brave front as they waved their children into an unknown future.

🐰🐰🐰

Tony pressed himself against the door of the train and leaned out of the window to keep Doris in sight. He bit his lip to hold in the panic when the guard blew his whistle, and the train began to move. The hiss of steam and the loud, slow *chuff, chuff* of the heaving engine muffled the shouts and cries of the waving children and their relatives. *Chuffity-chuff, chuffity-chuff*, the train began to speed up. Tony leaned out farther. His heart leapt when he saw Doris break away from the crowd and run along beside the train through the smoke and steam, waving her white hanky. He watched until she reached the end of the platform. She gave one last wave.

'Doris!' Tony shouted, but his voice was lost in the train's parting whistle and the faster *chuffity-chuff* rhythm. He felt limp, and wished he could lie down and wake up to find this was just a dream.

'Was that your mum, then?'

Tony turned to the girl pressed against him in the crush, watching the last of the crowd on the platform. He said nothing, biting back the tears.

'I'm *talking* to you,' she said, nudging Tony in the ribs.

She was about his own age. But, unlike everyone else, she looked cheerful. She was wearing a brown beret over two pigtails with red ribbons on the ends. Her brown coat was shabby and had patches on the elbows.

He wished she'd get lost.

'Your mum?' she asked again.

Tony wiped his nose on his sleeve. 'What's it to you?' he sniffed.

'Just asking,' she retorted. 'Nobody came to see me off,' she went on. 'My Aunty Bee was glad to get rid of me. She's not really my aunt. She's looked after me since my parents died of TB. Do you know what TB is?'

Tony shook his head. 'Is it some kind of bomb?'

'Bomb? No! It's a disease. First my mum got it, and then my father. That was years ago. I'm really glad of this war.'

*Glad?* he thought. *How can anyone be glad of all this war?* She was mad, this one.

'Yeah. Gets me away from skivvying for the old lady. Do you know, she makes me clear out the ashes every morning before I go to school – *and* peel spuds for her lodgers' dinner after I come home. Sick of it, I am. I'm dying to get to the country. I don't care if I have to sleep in a stable with smelly horses.'

'Will we have to do that?' asked Tony.

The girl laughed. 'We might have to do lots of things we don't like,' she said. 'But I don't care. Anything is better than working your knuckles off for an old bat who doesn't want you in the first place. You're lucky to have a pretty mum like that. I saw her chasing after the train. She really loves you, doesn't she?'

Tony sniffed, and tried to control his tears. He'd been down this road before, when his mam was put in a hole in the ground. You don't come back from a hole in the ground... but he'd go back to Doris and Da, he really would. The tears won. They flowed down his cheeks and ran down his nose and he didn't care who saw them.

'Aw,' the girl said. 'Leave off crying. You'll be back. Some boys on my street came back after a couple of weeks. It's just a laugh, all this. The gov'ment like to think they're looking after us young 'uns, but they're just messing with us, really. You'll be back in no time at all. Me, I'm going to ask whoever takes me on to let me stay for ever. And don't wipe your nose on your sleeve. That's disgusting, that is. Here, have my hanky. I nicked it from Aunty Bee's drawer.'

Tony took the hanky and wiped his face and nose. Then he offered it back to the girl.

'Yecchhh,' she laughed. 'You don't think I'm going to put that snotty thing back in my pocket, do you? You can keep it. Are those sandwiches in that tin?'

Tony clutched the precious tin of Bournville animals and shook his head. 'No, but I have some in my suitcase,' he said.

'Can I have some? I only have a slice of bread and marge.'

They squeezed on to a seat and he shared his sandwiches with the girl.

'My name is Alice.' she said. 'That's short for Mary Alice. But everyone calls me Alice. What's your name?'

'Tony.'

'That's an all right name. What's your mum called?'

Tony was thoughtful as he took another bite of his jam sandwich. 'Doris,' he said eventually. 'My mum's name is Doris.'

'Doris. That's an all right name too. You can travel with me, Tony. We'll look out for each other, you and me.'

Tony gripped his tin of animals closer. In one way, he wished this chattering girl would get lost. In another, he was glad she was with him.

'Yours is an all right name too,' he said, 'Alice.'

# CHAPTER TWELVE

Mallie's mum did think it over, and eventually agreed to give Steve's business proposition a go.

'Well, it's worth a try, Steve,' she said, when he brought a gingery hamster and two kittens over the following Tuesday. 'If nothing shifts after two weeks, we'll call it a day, OK?'

'Fine,' replied Steve. 'Though if the drawings don't get things moving, I don't know what will.' He turned to Mallie. 'Perhaps you'll bring these three back to the shop tomorrow when you come to work.'

Mallie looked tentatively at her mother. She was supposed to have worked out her notice the previous Saturday. Had Steve forgotten?

'If that's all right with you, Sarah.' he said, giving Mallie's mum a disarming grin. Just for a moment, Sarah Kelly looked embarrassed

'Of course it is,' she laughed.

The first three drawings sold with their posed pet models within a week. The following week, four were snapped up. Later on, there was a request from an old customer of Steve's father for a portrait of her elderly collie.

'A commission!' shrieked Mallie, when her mother told her. 'You get to go to people's houses and draw their pets? Mega, Mum! You've got it made. I knew you could do it. I knew that picture would inspire you. I really knew it would. It just leapt out at me as if it was meant for us – for you.'

Her mother laughed, as she crumbled a stock cube into a casserole. 'Looks like it,' she said. 'Thanks to you and Mrs H.' she added, nodding towards the picture on the dresser.

'Things are looking good,' Mallie told Jamila later. 'Now, when Steve brings pets for drawing, he stays for coffee. Mum has even made some of her oat biscuits. She says it's because she can do a bit of baking now that she's working in her own time. But I know she's doing it for Steve.'

'Ah, the old food-seduction trick,' said Jamila.

'The what?'

'My granny says it's the oldest trick in the game,' laughed Jamila. 'Goes right back to when Neanderthal women stirred up pan-fried mammoth and poached pterodactyl eggs to win over their hairy mates. Anyway, is everything going OK?'

'You bet,' said Mallie. 'Mum was easy. How could she refuse, seeing as she's on to such a good thing with those small animals?'

'And what about the old man? Is he giving you any grief?'

'Not much,' answered Mallie with a grin. 'He just frowned a bit when I arrived. Steve has obviously had a word with him. We're beginning to tolerate one another. At least he understands I'm not out to nick cash from his till.'

'Or release his stock into the wild,' added Jamila.

'Yeah,' Mallie smiled. 'Life's pretty OK right now.'

And life was to get even better.

'New CD, Mum?' said Mallie that evening, as her mother put the finishing touches to a charcoal sketch of a labrador puppy that was snoozing on the sofa.

Sarah smiled, and nodded towards the CD cover, *The Jazz Station*.

'Couldn't resist,' she said. 'Got it in the Oxfam shop. Louis Armstrong, "Blueberry Hill." One of Mum's favourites. Like it?'

'Cool,' said Mallie. It was good to see Mum happy again, even better that Gran was part of the bright atmosphere. 'You're doing well out of the sketches, aren't you?'

'Certainly am,' said her mum. 'Two more commissions for home drawings of pets – as well as what I'm doing for Steve. I owe you one, Mal. How about we celebrate?'

'Well, I was wondering,' began Mallie. 'Don't you think it might be a good idea to invite Steve for a meal? That way, we could all celebrate.'

Sarah mused, as she shaded in the puppy's eyes. 'Invite him here, you mean?'

'Yes, why not? A bit of excitement. It's been ages since we had people to eat with us. It used to be fun when...' She stopped, and bit her lip.

'When we had Simon's pals in for suppers? It's all right, Mallie, you can mention his name. What's past is past. Funny how they stopped coming. So, what are you suggesting, then?'

'Like I said, we'll cook a meal. What do you think?'

'Don't know,' said her mum doubtfully. 'Wouldn't it be simpler for all of us to go to the Pizza Palace?'

'Mum!' exclaimed Mallie. 'We want a bit of class. We want to impress. Let's do something from those dusty cookery books. Something with a fancy sauce and greenery sprinkled on top.' She paused, and frowned. 'Why are you smiling like that?'

Her mother shook her head and laughed, as she rubbed the puppy's shaded eye with her finger. 'Am I sensing something deeper here?' she asked.

Had Mum sussed her plan? 'What do you mean?'

Sarah glanced sideways at her daughter. 'Do I detect a bit of a crush here? A crush on Mister Steve?'

'MUM!' Mallie threw up her hands. 'Are you mental? A crush on Steve? How could you even *think* that?'

'Don't explode,' said her mum, holding out the sketch to see it from a distance. 'It happens. Young girls often get a crush on an older man. Me, I fell hook, line and sinker for my dentist when I was thirteen. Cost your gran a fortune in fillings.'

'You sad, sad thing, Mum,' laughed Mallie. 'I don't do crushes. Even the word is prehistoric.'

'OK,' said her mum. 'Let's talk about this meal.'

'Yes,' agreed Mallie. 'I just thought it would be a good business move – after all, he put you back into the human race. Gave you a living doing something you're good at.'

Sarah signed the finished drawing with a flourish and propped it against a vase. 'You're right,' she said. 'Let's go for it. I suppose we'd better ask his father too.'

Mallie wrinkled her nose. 'I hadn't planned on asking Old Thistle-pants,' she said. 'I thought… just the three of us, for a bit of a laugh.'

'It's his shop,' said her mum. 'It might have been Steve's idea to do the pet pictures, but it's still the old man's shop. I couldn't leave him out, could I? It would be unkind, Mal.'

''I suppose so,' said Mallie. There was no way out of it. She'd just have to put up with having the old man along too. At least her mum and Steve would get to know one another a bit better.

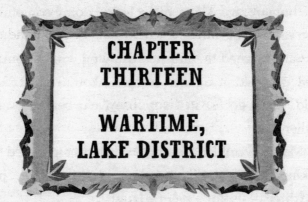

# CHAPTER THIRTEEN

# WARTIME, LAKE DISTRICT

'Do you know where you're going?' Alice asked Tony. They were standing in a queue of children lined up by Miss Gilmore and the teachers from other schools.

Tony shook his head. 'Me neither,' Alice went on. 'Look at all these people gaping at us. The others, at least, the ones not bawling their heads off, are saying silly things like they hope they'll get someone with a big house and garden and other children to play with. Me, I'll be happy if I get someone who likes a laugh and doesn't have lodgers who need their potatoes peeled. What about you, Tony? What sort of people are you hoping for?'

Tony shrugged. 'Don't care,' he said. 'I won't be staying long, anyway.'

'Ha,' laughed Alice. 'I'll be staying for ever.'

Some of the other teachers had begun handing youngsters over to the waiting adults. Miss Gilmore took Tony's arm.

'Your host is over here, Tony,' she said. 'Come on, lad,' she went on, as Tony shrank back. 'You be nice, now. These people are very good to take all you children away from the bombs.'

She led Tony to an elderly man standing beside a pony and trap. Under different circumstances – if Doris and his father had been with him – he'd have jumped at the chance of a ride in a pony and trap. But this was different.

'This is Mr Cregg,' Miss Gilmore said, still holding Tony by the arm. 'He and his wife have a nice farm. You'll like that, Tony.'

Tony glanced at the man's ruddy, weatherbeaten face and then focused his eyes on the ground, hoping he'd disappear.

Mr Cregg took off his battered hat as Miss Gilmore approached.

'This is Tony,' she said. 'Say hello to Mr Cregg, Tony.'

Tony raised his eyes for a second and nodded. Miss Gilmore prodded him.

'Hello, Mr Cregg,' he muttered.

'Small,' observed Mr Cregg.

'They're all small, Mr Cregg,' said Miss Gilmore. 'They're just children.'

Tony stood patiently, still focusing on the ground as Miss Gilmore wrote Mr Cregg's address in her folder. They chatted for a while, then Miss Gilmore turned to Tony.

'I'll give Mr Cregg's address to your father, Tony,' she said. 'Then you'll get lots of letters.' She gave him a reassuring smile and hurried off to attend to her other charges. Tony watched her, and wanted more than anything to run after her.

Mr Cregg opened the door of the trap and stood back. With a resigned sigh, Tony clambered up on board.

'I suppose you city youngsters know nothing about the countryside,' Mr Cregg said, climbing into the trap. Tony didn't know how to respond, so he said nothing. As the door of the trap snapped shut and the man shook the reins, Tony looked around desperately to see if anyone else would come running. His eyes sought out Alice, but there was no sign of her.

He sighed and, clutching his Bournville cocoa tin under one arm and his gas mask and string-bound suitcase under the other, sat back to meet the unknown.

He was surprised when they headed towards a great lake, and he was even more surprised when Mr Cregg got out and led the horse aboard a ferry that was filling up with farming folk carrying supplies. The wonder of crossing the lake – the gentle slap of the water, the chatting of the passengers and the splendid view of mountains, – washed away Tony's anxieties for a while. He marvelled at the scene – as if there was no past and no future, just this velvet calmness of now. It was only when he wished that his father and Doris could be here to see it, that he remembered why he was here. He looked at the faces of the people around him. Some of them nodded at him, but they seemed to know better than to ask questions of the dour Mr Cregg.

At the landing stage, Mr Cregg got out and guided the horse on to land. With a backward glance across the lake to where he'd left the only people he knew in this distant place, Tony resigned himself to being stuck with this granite-faced man. So apprehensive was he, that he scarcely noticed the rolling landscape they were passing through.

As they drove through a village, the man broke his silence.

'Near Sawrey,' he said.

Tony digested this for a moment. What was he supposed to say?

'Near where?' he asked.

The man looked at him and clucked his tongue. 'Not near anywhere, lad. This village is called Near Sawrey.'

If Tony thought this was a strange name for a place, or if there was a bigger place called Sawrey further on, he kept it to himself. When they eventually turned off the road on to a rough track through the trees, Tony could feel his isolation begin to reach panic level. He bit his lip to keep from crying out that he didn't want to go any further. The recent rain had turned the track into an oozing mire that slurped under the wheels of the trap.

Suddenly the dark trees gave way to a clearing in which stood a small stone cottage surrounded by sheds and barns. Welcoming smoke drifted lazily from a chimney. It was a comforting sight. Perhaps there might be cheerful people inside, even some children.

The front door opened and an elderly woman

in a white apron, her hair scraped back in a tight bun, emerged. As she scrutinised Tony, his optimism sank.

'This him, then?' she asked.

'It's him,' said her husband, opening the door of the trap. He nudged Tony out, clutching his Bournville tin and his suitcase.

'Lucky boy,' said the woman.

'Lucky?' said Tony. 'Why?'

'Why? Why? Lucky to be away from those bombs and that wrecked city, that's why.'

As he followed the woman into the house, Tony felt anything but lucky. More than anything he wanted to turn back, bombs or no bombs. The kitchen was warm, if a bit smoky. A kettle and a pot were steaming on the black range. Onions and herbs hung from a beam overhead.

'I expect you're hungry,' the woman said. 'Tony,' she added. 'We were told your name is Tony.' He nodded. 'Well, Tony, we serve simple fare here. Take what you're given and there'll be no trouble. There's a tap through there in the scullery where you can wash your hands.'

As he let the cold water run through his fingers, Tony gritted his teeth against any soft thoughts of home that would make him into a weepy sissy. He'd get through this. He'd make the most of it. Alice said that some of her friends had gone home after a short time. If he could just keep his head down and survive until then... maybe Hitler would be bombed and the war would be over in a few days. He took a deep breath and went back into the kitchen.

'Onion,' the woman said, as she ladled out some watery-looking soup. 'With a bit of potato to fatten you up. You can sit there.' She pointed to the chair nearest the window. 'Father will say grace.'

Tony bowed his head as the old man prayed, and waited patiently for the *Amen*. Then he eagerly downed the soup and cheese that followed. There wasn't much conversation. Apart from a few questions about conditions in London and the old couple's comments about sheep and farm business, the meal was accompanied only by the ticking of the clock on the dresser. *If Doris was here*, thought Tony, *we'd both be giggling helplessly*. Doris always said that the best belly-laughs were the ones when you weren't supposed to laugh, like in church or when someone farted during an arithmetic test. But he mustn't think of Doris.

'That was nice, thank you, missus,' he said.

'Well, you did it justice,' said the woman. 'Always a good sign, that.'

'Good lad,' said the man. 'I like a chap with manners. You'll do,' he added, with a chuckle. 'Now, you can come with me and I'll show you around the farm.'

Tony breathed a sigh of relief. They were human after all! He looked forward to seeing the farm. He had only vague recollections of visiting his mother's cousin's farm back in Ireland, but he did remember it as a happy time. He stepped warily over the mud as he followed the farmer across the yard.

The smell in the cowshed made him gag. The man laughed.

'You'll soon get used to that,' he said. 'We'll make a farmer of you yet.'

*I don't want to be a farmer,* thought Tony. But he responded politely to the chicken-run, the pigsty, the haybarn and the woodshed.

'Now you know where everything is,' the man said, as they went back to the house. Tony couldn't quite see the point of knowing where everything was. He was to find out soon enough.

Early next morning, there was a loud knocking on the door of the small room he'd been given.

'Rise and shine,' called the old man. 'Milking time.'

Milking time? Tony looked at the curtains. It was still dark outside. Maybe the man was knocking on some other door – the door of a farm labourer, perhaps? But the knocking beat again on Tony's door.

'Are you awake, lad?'

'Yes,' replied Tony.

'Come on, then, shake a leg, there's a good lad.'

The bed squeaked as Tony climbed out from under the patchwork quilt. He dressed and went sleepily down the stairs. The old man was putting on heavy-looking clogs. He nodded towards another pair of clogs by the range, their metal toe-caps and wooden soles spattered with dried mud.

'Try those for size,' he said. 'Used to belong to our Albert.'

Tony took off his shoes and eased his feet warily into the clumpy clogs. Who was 'our Albert', he wondered. Their son? The clogs felt lumpy and alien.

'They're a bit big,' he said.

Mr Cregg laughed. 'Never mind. An extra pair of socks will pad them out. Now, get your coat on and we'll go and fetch those cows.'

Tony shivered against the early morning chill. Daylight was slowly beginning to emerge from beyond the distant hill, giving barely enough light to make out the outlines of the sheds. He stumbled in the oversize clogs as he followed the old man across the muddy yard.

'You'll get used to this,' said Mr Cregg. 'A few days, and you'll know the way blindfold.'

Tony grimaced. He didn't want to know the way, blindfold or otherwise. He didn't want anything to do with this place. Mr Cregg pushed open a high wooden gate.

'You stand there,' he said to Tony, pointing to a spot beside the open gate. 'Some of these ladies like to wander, so you can whoosh them into line.' Then, with several 'hups', he went into the field. Tony watched with dread as the herd came towards him. He heard the slurp of their hooves in the mud and their heavy breathing as they loomed into sight. They were big!

Tony leapt behind the open gate as the

heavy creatures rumbled in from the field. Two of them broke away from the herd and veered to the left.

'What did I tell you?' shouted Mr Cregg from behind them. 'You didn't whoosh them into line, boy! You have to whoosh them into line, those new ones. Come out of there. Fat lot of use you'll be, if you're just going to hide.'

Tony came reluctantly out of his safe place and watched as Mr Cregg rounded up the wanderers. Together they followed the herd down to the farmyard and into the cowshed. Mr Cregg ushered the cows into individual stalls and tethered them.

'Now I'll show you how to milk,' said Mr Cregg, pulling up a low stool.

'No!' said Tony. 'I don't want to do that, Mister Cregg.'

Mr Cregg sighed and shook his head. 'You city folk,' he muttered. 'Look, my son should be here helping me – but he's out there fighting for his country. So I'm left to do all this on my own. You'll have to help. You can't expect me and Mrs Cregg to keep you here unless you're prepared to help, can you?'

At last, a way out. 'Then it might be better if

I went to someone else,' Tony volunteered. 'I don't know anything about farming, Mister Cregg. Best you get someone who does.'

Mr Cregg laughed. 'And how would I find a city boy who knows a bit about farming? I don't think so. You're stuck with us, lad. And we're stuck with you, so you'd best knuckle down and learn something about country life. Now, you grab this teat and we'll make a start.'

Tony swallowed hard and gingerly took the teat, closing his eyes to blot out the enormous rump and swishy tail of the cow. *Bombs*, he prayed. *Please let the bombing move to somewhere else, and then we can all go back to London, me and Alice and all those crying children from the train.*

# CHAPTER FOURTEEN

Old Mr Armstrong was in the shop when Mallie arrived after school. She glanced around. There was no sign of Steve.

'He's not here,' said Mr Armstrong.

'When will he be back?' asked Mallie.

'Later,' he replied.

They eyed one another warily for a while as Mallie fixed up the small-pet boxes in the window. More cute labrador puppies.

'I'm going to play some music,' Mr Armstrong said brusquely. 'Keeps the animals happy.'

'That's good,' Mallie said, not quite knowing how

she was supposed to react.

'Just telling you,' went on Mr Armstrong, feeding a disc into the CD player, 'so that you won't be making faces at my choice of music. There'll be none of your modern rubbish.'

*My modern rubbish,* Mallie thought crossly. This old man was going to do her head in, he really was. But she kept the thought to herself and waited for some boring old tune to float across the shop. She was pleasantly surprised by the sound she heard.

'It's Duke Ellington,' she said, turning to look at the old man.

His eyebrows shot up his forehead with amazement. 'You know Duke?'

'Yes,' replied Mallie, climbing out of the window. 'I love his "It don't mean a thing if it ain't got swing." And Ella Fitzgerald. I like her too. And Dizzy Gillespie...'

'Amazing,' said Mr Armstrong, turning down the sound.

'What's so amazing?' said Mallie. 'I like heaps of music. Where's the wonder in that? My mum plays jazz all the time at home. And my gran played it all the time when she was with us. I used to sit on her lap and she'd jog me up and down in time to the music.

She was an artist, just like Mum. She drew animals, too...'

Mallie broke off. She hadn't spoken about her granny to anyone for years, but somehow it seemed all right to mention her to the old man. Maybe it was the fact that he was actually being civil that made her prattle on.

'Another artist in the family, then,' he said. 'Are her animals as good as your mother's?'

Mallie took a deep breath. 'I think so,' she replied. 'Mum packed away all Gran's pictures when she died. It makes her too sad...'

'Oh, I see,' said Mr Armstrong. 'I'm sorry.'

Mallie shrugged. 'Yes, well...' she began, suddenly embarrassed. She nodded towards the CD player. 'Are you going to turn up the music, Mr Armstrong?'

Mallie was busy for the rest of the afternoon. It was about four o'clock when Mr Armstrong emerged from the back of the shop with two mugs of coffee and a half-packet of biscuits.

'Time for a break,' he said.

Mallie was surprised, but she tried not to show it.

Mr Armstrong smiled at her. 'How refreshing,' he said.

'What is?'

'To meet someone so young who likes my sort of music.'

'Like I said, Mr Armstrong,' Mallie said, 'Mum and me like jazz best when we're together. I suppose it's a kind of a bond – a generation bond, maybe. Music has nothing to do with age. Mum says that Beethoven would have liked jazz if he'd hung around long enough.'

'And you really like Duke Ellington?'

Mallie nodded. Would he ever leave off the music questions? But at least it gave them something to talk about. Better than having him glaring at her from under his hairy eyebrows.

'I have some old seventy-eights in the attic,' Mr Armstrong went on, warming to his subject. 'I could show them to you, if you like.'

'Seventy-eights?'

'Old records. The originals – before vinyls and these modern CD things.'

'Really? Great.'

'Yes, but you'll have to go up to the attic yourself, girl. My busted leg and all that.'

So Mallie found herself armed with a torch and climbing a ladder into the attic above the landing.

'What if a customer comes in?' she asked Mr Armstrong.

'I'll hear the bell. That's it, push up the trapdoor. Now, pull yourself in, and the records should be on your left.'

Mallie gasped at the dusty smell of old things heaped in the overcrowded attic. Shining the torch around, she saw a bundle of square record sleeves. Duke Ellington, Benny Goodman, Louis Armstrong – could he be a dark-skinned relation? She smiled at the thought, trying to imagine the grinning duke and the crusty man at the bottom of the ladder side by side.

'What's keeping you, Mallie? Can you see them?' came a muffled voice from below.

Mallie tucked three records under her arm and began her precarious descent.

'Here,' said Mr Armstrong, reaching up. 'Pass me the records, in case you drop them. Careful, now. We don't want the two of us hobbling about with busted legs.' He chuckled.

She passed him the records and the torch, and swung herself down. Mr Armstrong dusted the record covers with his sleeve.

'Haven't seen these for years,' he said with a smile. 'Not since Steve stashed them up there when

I moved. It's good that you started me talking about them. Now I have an excuse to listen.'

'On what?' asked Mallie.

'What do you mean?'

'Well, they're old,' explained Mallie. 'Do you have an old-fashioned record player?'

Mr Armstrong scratched his head and gave a sheepish grin. 'Silly me,' he said. 'I don't. Oh well, I won't ask you to carry them all the way back. I'll keep them where I can look at them now and then. Here, you take them into the shop while I put up this ladder.'

Steve arrived back shortly afterwards. He was wearing a trendy leather jacket and a tie. *He scrubs up well*, thought Mallie approvingly. Couldn't have Mum falling for scruff. He was looking pleased with himself.

'Well?' said his father.

'All set,' replied Steve. 'Starting in October.'

'OK,' muttered Mr Armstrong. 'Well, at least it will give you time to ease me back into full labour.'

Steve's face fell slightly as he nodded at Mallie and disappeared into the back of the shop. Mallie looked questioningly at the old man.

'He's got a job,' he explained. 'Lecturing.'

'Where?' asked Mallie, her heart sinking. Was Steve going to disappear out of their lives before he and Mum had had a chance to get together? No romance? She sighed. She should have known better than listen to Jamila. Real life doesn't work out like that. Jamila and her Mills and Boon philosophy!

'Where is he going?'

'Veterinary college,' said Mr Armstrong.

'Oh, great,' enthused Mallie. The veterinary college, attached to the university, was just fifteen miles away. Near enough for the aura of romance to stay within reach. Maybe there was hope after all.

'Fancy stuff,' grumbled Mr Armstrong. 'Lecturing about big creatures that we never even see here in this country. Why couldn't he have settled for regular veterinary medicine? When he was little, I used to take him everywhere with me. He always loved small animals – just as I did. But no, he had to go fancy, didn't he?'

'You mean, you're not proud of him?' asked Mallie in surprise. 'I'd be dead proud if someone belonging to me was able to lecture on animals – any kind of animals.'

'Hmm,' muttered Mr Armstrong again, hairy eyebrows coming together above his nose.

*Thorny old git*, thought Mallie. The short, pleasant interlude was over and he was back to his barking. *And*, she gritted her teeth, *he probably wouldn't approve of Mum*. He'd probably give her a hard time if she and Steve got together. *Well, I'm damned if I'm going to let him go down that road.*

The words were out before she realised: 'You're a real moaner, you are, Mr Armstrong. You're only thinking of yourself.' She glanced warily at the old man, expecting a tirade of abuse, or an old-person lecture on youngsters giving lip.

To her surprise, he didn't do either.

'Steve and I,' he said, 'we have our own way of communicating. He knows I'm proud of him.'

'How could he know that? Isn't it much easier to use the right words rather than mumble negative stuff like that? I certainly wouldn't know what someone meant if they *hmpfed* and growled like you do.'

'You're a proper little madam,' said Mr Armstrong. 'If it wasn't for your love of jazz, I'd have you out of the door.' But he was smiling as he said it.

'If it wasn't for the fact that you're sometimes nearly human, I'd be *gone* out of the door,' she retorted.

Mr Armstrong chuckled at that. What a difference

127

it made to his face, Mallie observed – like a wrinkled prune that's suddenly plumped up! She was gratified, when Steve returned to the shop, to see Mr Armstrong pat him on the back and say, 'Well done, lad,' and wink across at her.

They both responded enthusiastically to her invitation to supper.

# CHAPTER FIFTEEN

# WARTIME, LAKE DISTRICT

Evening. With the milking over there were no more chores, apart from herding the cows back to their pasture. This was the time of day Tony liked best. Mrs Cregg packed bread and cheese and a bottle of fresh milk for him and, once the cows were safely back to grazing, he was free to roam the hills until dusk. It was a mutual arrangement. He knew the Creggs liked to talk in the evenings, and he felt awkward in their company, as no doubt they felt in his. So his suggestion that he'd like to look around was met with enthusiasm, along with warnings not to go too far and to hurry back if he heard the sound of planes.

'It's because we're near the coast, lad,' explained Mr Cregg. 'We get planes flying over the coast.'

Tony loved the names of the places that surrounded the Cregg farm. There was Hawkshead, where he sometimes went shopping with the Creggs in their horse and trap. Mr Cregg had even let him hold the reins a few times. 'Hawkshead,' he said softly, as he climbed over the gate. 'Sawrey, Near Sawrey, Far Sawrey.' He chuckled. Really nice names. He could almost see his dad and Doris smiling when he'd tell them about these quiet places tucked away across a wide lake called Windermere.

'Hup, Cowslip,' he said, as he passed the grazing cows in the meadow. He'd got used to the creatures and called each of them affectionately by name. He liked the sweet smell of their warm breath and the way they twitched their velvet ears. Although he had to work hard from morning to evening, he was becoming used to the routine. While gathering eggs, checking the sheep, cleaning out the pigsty, mending the stone walls with Mr Cregg and milking the cows, he had the July evenings to look forward to. He wished he knew more about country life, but he was quite happy just to explore. *This evening I'll head towards Near Sawrey*, he thought. It seemed as if he had the whole world to himself, as he crossed streams and ran down the hills that he could see from his bedroom window. Swallows swooped overhead and in the distance pheasants were calling. It was hard to think that down in London people would already be queuing to get into the public shelters, and that by now more buildings would be bombed out of existence. It didn't seem right that he could enjoy this freedom while his father and Doris were living in fear. He wished he could spirit them here. But that sort of despair wouldn't help, so he tried to concentrate on the things around him.

A small grove of trees across the field seemed like a good place to eat, so he climbed over some stone walls and made his way there. Nothing to hear except the swish of long grass as he moved through it. *Everyone should live in the country*, he thought. Then he giggled aloud at the prospect of millions of people dotted in cottages all over England. Mad, that'd be. All these fields would be full and there would be no stretches of land left like this.

He'd just settled under a tree and was about to sink his teeth into his cheese sandwich, when he heard voices. He froze. He'd heard stories of Nazis being shot down and hiding out in remote places.

What would he do if he came face-to-face with one? Should he hide, or should he be brave and confront him? *And do what? Challenge him to a duel? Pretend he had a gun and march him back to the village?* There was the voice again! Soft and whispery. It must be very close. Should he run for it? And get shot in the back – martyr to a country that Da said we weren't really part of? Though Tony could never really come to terms with that – he felt he belonged to England more than to any other place. He sighed, and wished Da was here. He quietly rewrapped his sandwich and put it and the bottle of milk back into his pocket. Then he stealthily made his way into the shrubbery. He could hide here.

Two voices now. He stopped – they were women's voices. *Are there women Nazis?* There could be. Mr Cooper back home had said he wouldn't put anything past a man with a funny moustache and bad haircut who saluted like a chimp reaching up for a banana.

Tony parted the leaves. Two females, one young and one old, had their backs to him. They were bent over something and talking in low voices. Then the younger one stood up and put her hands on her hips.

Tony blinked. Was he dreaming?

'Alice?' he cried, leaping from his hiding-place. 'It's you!'

Alice frowned. Then she recognised her evacuee travelling companion.

'Hey, missus,' she said, tapping the old woman's shoulder. 'It's Tony!'

The old woman turned and straightened up – though straightened was probably not quite accurate, as she had an old-age stoop. She was wearing a long skirt and a hat with a wide brim. She was holding something furry in her arms. As her keen eyes swept over him, Tony hesitated.

'Come along, boy,' she said. 'Let's see more of Alice's travelling companion. She's told me about you.'

'We don't bite,' giggled Alice. 'Tony, this is Mrs H. She's my friend.'

'Mrs H?' said Tony.

The old lady laughed as she held out her free hand. 'That's what Alice calls me,' she said. 'So you might as well call me that too. Nice and short. Come and see our rabbit.'

Rabbit? *They weren't trapping rabbits, were they?* Tony swallowed, as a fleeting memory of Joe Dolan flashed to mind. He stepped warily towards them.

'See?' said Alice, pointing to the furry bundle. 'We've rescued a rabbit.'

'Caught in a rabbit-snout, poor thing,' said the old lady.

'That's a trap,' explained Alice. 'Look,' she pointed to a hole in the stone wall. 'There's a hole left near the bottom of the wall. The rabbits go through and get caught in a snare. Me and Mrs H look out for the poor beggars.'

Tony looked at the hole. So *that* was why Mr Cregg always left an opening when he and Tony were repairing the stone walls that divided his land! Rabbit snouts. Tony resolved to patch them up in future.

'Luckily there are no bones broken, just a cut from the snare,' Mrs H was saying. 'We've cleaned it. We can let him go now, Alice. He'll heal nicely.'

Giving a pat to its brown head, Alice lifted the rabbit from Mrs H and put him on the ground. He sat for a moment, looking warily around him. Then, with a bound, he disappeared into the undergrowth. Alice let out a cheer. 'That's two this week,' she said. 'Isn't that right, Mrs H?'

Mrs H smiled, and nodded. 'Alice here has

a special way with animals,' she said. 'I couldn't have done it without her.'

Alice's face beamed with pride. 'See?' she said again. 'I'm doing real well in the country. How about you, Tony?'

Tony shrugged. 'I'm doing OK,' he replied. 'It's hard work, but I'm free every evening after the milking.'

'Milking?' Alice shrieked with laughter. 'That sounds like fun.'

'Huh, not when you've to get up at dawn,' Tony muttered. Then he listed his other chores. 'Look,' he added, holding out his calloused, dirt-ingrained hands.

Mrs H nodded sympathetically. 'Things are different in the country,' she said. 'Farm life is hard. But it has its rewards. Isn't it better than sheltering from bombs? Those poor people in London and along the coast, my heart goes out to them.' Then she looked at the two children, and realising she'd stirred up their fears, she said, 'Time for tea, I think.'

'Good,' said Alice, skipping ahead. 'I've been to Mrs H's cottage lots of times. She doesn't usually let children in, but I'm special. What about it, Mrs H? Can Tony come too?'

Mrs H peered at Tony and he shrank under her piercing eyes, shuffling his feet in the grass.

'So long as he doesn't touch things,' she said. 'I don't like children who touch things.'

'He won't touch a thing,' said Alice, with a shake of her head. 'I promise.'

As they made their way across the fields, Mrs H pointed out fox tracks, badger sets, the various breeds of cattle grazing in the fields and, when she came to her own spread, her flock of sheep.

'Herdwicks,' she said, leaning on the gate to admire them. 'I'm so proud of them.'

'Herdwicks?' said Alice, perched on the gate. 'I didn't know sheep had names. Sheep are just sheep.'

Mrs H laughed. 'You still have a lot to learn, Alice,' she said.

As they neared a house with a small porch, two small dogs ran excitedly to her. 'My pets,' she said. 'My little treasures. My foot-warmers.' And she bent to fuss over them as they jumped around her ankles.

They all ducked when a plane flew overhead. Mrs H looked up, shaking her head.

'I hate planes,' she said. 'I've always hated those noisy things. But I hate them even more now that they're on terrible killing missions.'

Tony shielded his eyes with his hand and gazed upwards. 'That's one of ours,' he said. 'Coming back from a mission. I know the markings.'

'I don't care whose it is,' muttered Mrs H. 'I hate them. I really do. Noisy and bent on death. Oh, I shudder for mankind. Let's have some tea, and we'll try to imagine there's no war. We'll sit out here on the garden seat.'

Tony took out his squashed sandwich and bottle of milk and put them on a small stone table. 'You can share my supper,' he said.

'I think we can add a little to that.' Mrs H smiled. 'I have biscuits. Nobody else in all of England has biscuits like these.'

'Real biscuits?' exclaimed Alice.

Mrs H tapped her nose. 'I get presents from friends in America,' she laughed. 'Now, sit down, you two. I'll call when I want you to carry the tea things out.'

When she'd gone into her cottage, Tony and Alice looked at one another.

'This is as far as we get,' giggled Alice. 'Sometimes she lets me inside, but mostly we sit out here. She has no children of her own, so she thinks we all do nothing else except muck up houses. But I'm gradually teaching her, so don't you go spilling things or slobbering, or touching any of that garden stuff, OK?'

Tony nodded. 'I'm really glad to see you, Tony,' Alice went on. 'I looked around for you at the station, but you'd gone.'

'I looked around for you, too,' said Tony. 'How come you weren't on the ferry?'

'Some mix-up,' snorted Alice. 'My people were late coming to pick me up. Miss Gilmore nearly danced a jig, she was that worried. I think she thought she'd have to haul me back to London with her.' She laughed. 'But anyway, they came and we got a later ferry. I didn't even know you'd come across the lake. We must be the only ones who did. Do you know the name of the lake?'

'Course I do,' said Tony. 'Windermere.'

'Windermere,' said Alice. 'Lake Windermere. Isn't that a dead nice name, Tony?'

# CHAPTER SIXTEEN

'It's seven o'clock, Mum,' said Mallie. 'They'll be here at seven-thirty.'

'No panic, Mallie,' said her mum. 'Everything is doing nicely.'

'I know, but shouldn't you be getting ready? You don't want to be red-faced and sweaty when they arrive. You should be relaxing with a glass of wine when they come – just like a regular hostess.'

'Hostess!' laughed her mum. 'We're not running a dodgy night-club here, Mal. And would you mind telling me what the candles are in aid of?'

'Atmosphere,' said Mallie. 'There's the bell. They're here!'

Sarah laughed as she went to answer the door. Mallie wished her mum had dressed in something more becoming than that multi-coloured baggy cardigan which looked like she'd slept in it – which she had been known to do when the heating oil ran out.

At first, everyone was a bit formal. Even Mr Armstrong was struggling with polite chit-chat, as he perched uncomfortably on the clean throw Mallie had put over the armchair. However, after a while the conversation loosened up and by the time dinner was ready, the words were flowing.

'I'll serve, Mum,' said Mallie. 'You sit and chat.' Good. Mum and Steve were really hitting it off. Mr Armstrong was more interested in the collection of CDs.

Mallie felt warm and content as she set the best dinner plates on the green placemats and strained the bits of cork out of the wine bottle. She scraped the burnt bits off the garlic bread and announced dinner. The presence of two tall guests made the kitchen seem tiny, but at least nobody's elbows were up against the dresser. Mallie took the casserole out of the oven and placed it in the centre of the table.

'Ta-ra!' she said, as she lifted off the lid. *'Boeuf Stroganoff!'*

'Smells good,' enthused her mum.

'Beef?' said Mr Armstrong.

*'Boeuf Stroganoff,'* said Mallie again.

There was an awkward silence. Mallie glanced at her mum, who raised her eyebrows slightly.

'We don't eat m...' began Mr Armstrong.

'It's all right, Dad,' interrupted Steve, looking embarrassed. 'It will be fine,' he went on, looking at Sarah. 'It smells delicious and I'll certainly have some.'

'You're vegetarians?' said Sarah, ladle poised over the steaming casserole.

'Yes,' replied Mr Armstrong. 'Both of us. Gave up meat when Steve was a small lad and figured out that meat came from the sort of animals we treated on farms. You remember, Steve? That calf with the velvety ears...'

'It's all right, Dad,' put in Steve. 'Let's not go into that. We'd love to have your casserole, Mallie. I insist.'

Sarah put down the ladle. 'No, no,' she said, replacing the lid. 'Never mind. Mallie and I will share it tomorrow. Meanwhile, let's dig into the salads and garlic bread. Please,' she added, when Steve began to protest. 'No harm done.'

*No harm done?* Mallie's jaw dropped. After all her trouble! She glared at Steve. That was the whole dinner party ruined.

'Sorry, Mallie,' he said, noting Mallie's expression.

'I said *dinner*, didn't I?' muttered Mallie.

'Supper, Mallie,' said Steve. 'You said supper. I thought we were just coming for sandwiches and buns.'

'It doesn't matter,' put in Sarah. 'Saves us cooking a meal tomorrow. Now, who's for garlic bread – while it's still hot?'

Conversation was a bit strained for a while. Mallie felt deflated. She'd made her mum buy the best beef. She was hurt on her mum's behalf and angry with herself for screwing up. She knew she had said 'supper' – she'd figured that 'dinner' sounded too poncy, and had tried to keep the invitation casual. *I should have known*, she thought. *I should have known it was too good to be true.* However, when she produced the Strawberry Pavlova, things improved. By the time the first wine bottle was empty the chat was flowing again, and Sarah brought out a second bottle.

'No, no, really, we've had enough wine,' protested

Steve, glancing meaningfully at his father.

Mr Armstrong waved a skinny hand. 'Tosh, Steve. We're having a good time. Give it a rest.'

'Dad,' began Steve. But Mr Armstrong was holding out his glass. Mallie noted Steve's grim face and wondered at this puritanical attitude. What harm was the old man doing, having another glass of wine?

She was soon to find out. As he downed more wine, Mr Armstrong became more vociferous, dominating the conversation and constantly making joyful interruptions. Steve was clearly embarrassed.

'I think it's time for us to go,' he said, looking at his watch. Mallie knew it didn't matter what time was on the watch, Steve was simply putting on a polite act. Her mum nodded. But Mallie didn't want it to end like this. 'We haven't had coffee yet,' she said. 'Real coffee,' she added, looking pleadingly at Steve. 'We watched it being ground.'

Steve smiled, and looked meaningfully at Sarah. She picked up on his predicament and put her hand on Mallie's shoulder. 'Another time, Mallie,' she whispered soothingly. 'Steve will come back soon, won't you?'

'Love to,' said Steve, looking relieved. 'I'll hold you to that, Sarah.'

But Mallie wasn't convinced. This whole idea had been a disaster. Why did she ever listen to Jamila? There was no way Mum and Steve were ever going to get together now.

She glared at Mr Armstrong, who was being reluctantly helped from his chair by Steve. As he swung his elbow away from his son, he turned to face the dresser. He froze. His face lost its tipsy expression and the hairy eyebrows drew together.

'That... that picture,' he spluttered, looking at the drawing that Mallie had bought her mum.

'Isn't it lovely?' said Sarah indulgently. 'It shouldn't be here. I normally keep it in pride of place on the living-room mantelpiece. Mallie gave it to me for my birthday.'

'That's *my* picture,' put in Mr Armstrong. Then he turned his attention to Mallie.'Where did you get that picture?' he asked accusingly.

Mallie was taken aback by the intensity of his tone. 'I bought it,' she replied. 'In an antique...'

'Bought it?' the old man raised his voice. 'Bought it! You couldn't have done, Mallie. That's my picture. You nicked it from the attic, didn't you? When I sent you up for the jazz records...'

'That's enough, Dad,' put in Steve sternly, grasping

his father's arm. 'It's time we went home. Come on.'

'I won't go home without my picture,' protested his father. 'That's my precious picture.'

'Hold on.' Sarah pushed herself in front of Mallie. 'I think you're going a bit far, Mr Armstrong,' she said. 'Mallie bought this picture for me for my birthday. I don't see how you can imagine it's…'

'It's *my* picture! I'm telling you. How did you come by it?'

*Dad!*' Steve said angrily. 'Stop this now. You have no right…'

'I have every right,' retorted his father. 'It's my picture.' He lowered his voice. 'From Mrs H,' he mumbled. 'Mrs H's picture.' Neither Steve nor Sarah heard his mumbling. But Mallie did.

'I'm so sorry, Sarah,' Steve said. 'I don't know where he got this idea.'

'Oh, never mind, Steve,' said Sarah. 'I'm sure he'll be fine once you get him home.'

Steve led his father, still protesting loudly, to the door. 'I'm terribly sorry,' said Steve again, turning back towards Mallie and her mum. 'It… it's the drink, you see. He can't handle it. He's still on medication and shouldn't have alcohol. It's my fault, Sarah. But it's so long since I've seen him enjoy himself…'

'Don't worry, Steve,' said Sarah. 'Thank you for coming.' She waved, then gently closed the door when she heard the car doors close.

'Whew,' she said to Mallie. 'That was a barrel of laughs, Mallie.' Then: 'What's wrong, honey? You look like you've seen the proverbial ghost. You're not taking a poor, tipsy man's ramblings to heart, are you? You heard what Steve said. The old man can't hold wine and medication together. Some foggy memory was stirred up by that picture, and he thought it was his. Don't take any notice. He'll die of shame when he sobers up. Except that we won't be around to see it.'

'What do you mean, Mum?' asked Mallie.

'Let's give them a rest for a while – just to let the embarrassment cool down,' replied her mum. 'Then both sides can consider whether to continue – or not.'

'I know by your tone that you're going for the "or not", aren't you, Mum?'

Sarah shrugged. 'Damned if I'm going to do work for someone who accuses my daughter of nicking things. And you should give the place a wide berth, too, honey. This time, I really do insist. I'll phone Steve and tell him we're taking a little break. We've enough to contend with, without inviting extra baggage like that. Anyway, Steve is there to help in the shop before he starts lecturing.'

*Oh, great,* Mallie groaned to herself. *Everything – my job, Mum's job and the Great Romance – bites the dust.*

# CHAPTER SEVENTEEN
## WARTIME, LAKE DISTRICT

'Off to see the countryside again?' said Mrs Cregg, slicing cheese. 'You must know it inside out by now.'

Tony said nothing, just nodded. He hadn't told the Creggs about his visits across the fields to Mrs H's farm during the past couple of weeks. Best not to, in case they put a stop to it. They were people who kept to themselves, and he intuitively felt they would probably want him to do the same. The evening meetings with Mrs H and Alice were what kept him sane in this lonely place, and he wasn't about to jeopardise that.

Mrs H knew every hill and wood for miles around,

and she would tell Tony and Alice stories about the Lake District. Once she pointed out a distant strip of land at the edge of Lake Windermere.

'I saved that bit of foreshore,' she said proudly.

'Saved it? How?' asked Alice. 'How do you save something like that? What's there to save it from?'

'Developers,' replied Mrs H. 'They wanted to build there. Can you imagine it, churning up that lovely place to fill it with terraces of silly little houses?'

'I wouldn't mind,' said Alice. 'I'd love to have a house right there. Houses should be in pretty places, Mrs H.'

Mrs H tut-tutted and shook her head.

'How did you save it?' put in Tony, before Alice could start an argument.

'Oh, I raised some money,' she said with a smile. 'I painted some pictures and sold them. They made enough money to save that stretch of land.'

'Cor,' said Alice. 'Are you a real artist, Mrs H?'

Mrs H chuckled. 'Oh, I've been known to dabble a bit, dear. I don't have time for that sort of thing now. Farming is a busy life. Now, come along, you two. Best turn back before the evening closes in.'

The walks always ended in the garden with tea and scones, or biscuits from America.

'You know, I don't actually live in this cottage,' she said to them one evening. 'I used to live here, but now I live in another house not far from here.'

'But you're always here, Mrs H,' said Alice. 'It's got rooms and furniture and everything. We've always ended up here in the evenings, me and you.'

Mrs H laughed. 'Oh, I still own it. It's still my special place. I like to sit here in the evenings.'

'Evenings? That's mad,' said Alice with a laugh. 'Why would anyone want two houses?'

Mrs H simply smiled. 'It's this garden,' she said. 'Its peace shuts out wars and woes.'

However, it was her love of animals that drew Tony to Mrs H. He found it easy to tell her about his mother and the rabbits.

'It was a picture in her bedroom,' he said. 'A picture of rabbits in a field. There were hills behind them and some trees, a bit like here. I can still remember every detail in that picture. My mam used to tell me that we'd go there some day. I never forgot that. I suppose that's why I love rabbits.'

He glanced shyly at Mrs H and Alice to see if they'd laugh. But they didn't. Mrs H nodded.

'My brother and I used to catch rabbits and tame

them,' she said. 'When he was sent away to school, I used to do it on my own. You're never lonely with animals around you.'

'That's true,' said Tony. 'Even tin ones,' he laughed. 'I'll show you my collection.'

'And did she take you to see the rabbits, your mother?' Alice asked Tony.

He shook his head. 'She died,' he said. 'When I was small.'

Alice snorted. 'Liar, liar, pants on fire,' she said. 'Your mum's a pretty lady who saw you off at the station. Her name is Doris. You told me so yourself.'

Tony flinched. He'd forgotten that he'd fibbed to Alice. 'She's my father's friend,' he said. 'And mine too. She's a bit like a mother, but not my real mother.'

'You could have said,' went on Alice, wagging her finger at him. 'I don't like liars.'

'It was too much trouble to try and explain,' muttered Tony.

Mrs H diverted their attention by opening a book she had brought out. 'This is about the countryside,' she said. 'You might find it interesting.'

As she opened it, a sheet of paper fell to the floor. Alice picked it up.

'That's nice,' she said. 'A picture of mice.'

'That's one of my first drawings,' Mrs H said, smiling. 'I did that when I was eleven. I keep it here because it's special.'

Alice examined it more closely. 'You drew that?' she exclaimed. 'That's amazing.'

The old lady smiled. 'As I've said already, Alice, I'm just a sheep farmer who used to draw.'

'I wish I could draw like that,' went on Alice.

'Perhaps you could,' said Mrs H. 'You never know until you try.'

Alice shook her head. 'I don't have a pencil or paper,' she said.

Mrs H laughed. 'I can provide,' she said. 'Before you leave, I'll give you some drawing materials.'

Later, as the sun began to sink, Mrs H ushered the two youngsters away.

'You want to be home before those wretched planes start their droning,' she said, looking up at the sky. 'Go straight home now, no dallying' – just as she said every evening.

Alice decided to accompany Tony some of the way across the fields, instead of saying goodbye as they usually did at Mrs H's gate.

'Imagine we're only a few fields apart,' said Alice,

a sketchbook and pencil case tucked under her arm. 'I'm really glad you're near, Tony.'

'Me too,' said Tony. 'What are the people like, where you're staying?'

'The Taylors. They're all right. I help them a bit, but it's only easy things like setting the table and playing with their baby. And they have a gramophone that they let me play. I like it there, but I don't think they'll keep me for ever. I suppose I'll have to go back to crabby Abby.'

Tony grinned. 'You didn't really think you'd get away that easily, did you? There are laws about guardians and things.'

Alice shrugged. 'I'm an optimist, me. Mrs H told me so. I live in hope.'

'Hope of what?'

'Hope that I'll get away as soon as I can, and work hard to make something of myself. I don't want to end up cleaning rooms and peeling potatoes for the rest of my life. Not me.'

Tony looked at the determined set of Alice's jaw. 'You *will* make something of yourself,' he said.

'Do you think so?' Alice stopped. 'Do you really think so, or are you just being a flatterer?'

'Of course I think so. I only ever told a lie once –

and you know about that one,' he added with a grin.

Alice changed direction and headed towards a gap in a hedge. 'This is where I go,' she said. 'My farm is just over the far side. See the smoke from the chimney? Funny, the way farmers keep fires going in summer.'

'Because they cook on ranges, I suppose,' said Tony. 'I like the smoke. I like the way it curls up to the sky. Dreamy and comforting.'

Alice laughed, just before she ducked into the gap. 'Bit of a poet, aren't you, Tony? See you tomorrow? I'll wait at that crooked tree at seven o'clock. That's after I've helped put the baby to bed. And you'll have finished the milking.'

'Yes. See you then,' said Tony.

He ran through the last two fields. The past few weeks had pushed the war farther away. The letters from his father and Doris were cheerful and, although he knew they were putting up a cheerful front for him, he clung to their optimism to quell his feelings of guilt at being so happy with Alice and Mrs H, while bombing raids still engulfed London.

When he let himself into the farmhouse,

Mrs Cregg met him with a worried face.

'You're late,' she said. 'Father's taken a chill, so you'll have to do some extra work for the next few days. No more evening rambles for a while.'

# CHAPTER EIGHTEEN

'It was awful,' Mallie groaned to Jamila the next day, as they sat over two cappucinos in the shopping centre. 'You wouldn't believe just how awful it was. Can you imagine? I felt such a twit, taking the lid off the casserole and saying, "Ta-ra!"'

'You actually said that?'

'Oh, don't make it worse, Jamila. I was so pleased that everything was going well, I was in a real "Ta-ra!" mood. And then there was that awful silence. I still cringe at the memory. I wish I could get amnesia and forget the whole mess.'

'I could hit you on the head with a heavy stone,' offered Jamila. 'Or a hunk of frozen beef,' she added with a giggle. 'Boeuf knock-it-off. That would blank the memory.'

'Thanks, Jam,' muttered Mallie.

'I'm sorry, Mallie,' said Jamila contritely. 'Anyway, it's him accusing you of stealing that picture that gets me. That's weird, that is.'

Mallie frowned thoughtfully. 'That's the thing,' she said. 'That's what's doing my head in. It's weird.'

'That's what I've just said.'

'No,' continued Mallie. 'I mean *really* weird. It's something the old man mumbled. Something that Mum or Steve didn't seem to hear.'

'Yes? Go on. What did he mumble?'

'"Mrs H." He mumbled, "Mrs H's picture." That's what he said.'

'So?' asked Jamila.

'Don't you see? He couldn't have known about the writing on the back of the picture unless he had seen it before.'

'And what was the writing?' queried Jamila. 'Remind me, Mallie. I'm beginning to feel like Alice in Wonderland here.'

'Don't you remember?' said Mallie. 'There's a scruffy label stuck on the back of the picture with faded writing on it. It says, "Mrs H's picture."'

Jamila shrugged. 'Don't remember that. But, if you say so.'

'It was – it is. I can show it to you. How could old Mr Armstrong have known? That's what bothers me most.'

'See?' said Jamila. 'I knew you should have stuck with the rings and bracelets.'

Mallie gave Jamila a withering look. 'I hate it when you do that.'

'What? What have I done?'

'Put on that snooty, I-told-you-so face. It's so annoying.'

'Especially when it's true,' laughed Jamila. 'No point in blaming me for the bad vibes.'

'Bad vibes?' echoed Mallie. 'Bad earthquake, more like. Disastrous dinner, embarrassing row... accusations of theft. Look.' She turned her face to Jamila. 'See these bags under my eyes. You could fly to America with a load of luggage that would fit into these bags. I haven't slept all night.'

'And what about the animal pictures?' asked Jamila. 'The ones that have made your mum human again?'

'Oh, all that's on hold,' said Mallie bitterly. 'I might have known something so good wouldn't last. And I'm banned from going there by Mum – not that I wanted to go,' she added hastily. 'Me being a thief and all. I couldn't face going back.'

'So, cancel the wedding planner, then?' said Jamila.

'Wedding? Ha! Don't make me laugh. No, it's just like it always was, except that this time I really felt it would work, with Mum doing the sort of thing that she's well qualified to do. She was always drawing little animal pictures for me when I was a kid. She could have done smashing books...'

'Until she got sidetracked into weird art,' put in Jamila. 'I know. You've told me. Many times.'

Mallie nodded, as she idly stirred the foam from the sides of her cup. 'I think it was because she didn't want to be an imitation of her own mother. Gran did all that sort of stuff. So, now we're back to square one, Jam. Except that now I'm extra depressed because I've no job. Though what really bugs me is how that old man seemed to know the picture.'

'Look,' said Jamila. 'I'm tired of the whole dreary saga. *So* it hasn't worked out between your mum and Steve. *So* she has to look for another job. *So* love has sunk over the horizon. It's no worse than it was before. Get over it, Mallie, eh?'

Later that evening, Mallie and her mother were watching television.

'Do you really have to give up your job, Mum?' Mallie said, during the advertisements.

Sarah Kelly shook her head and brushed crumbs from her lap. 'Let's just cool it for a while, Mal.'

And there was nothing more to be discussed.

Then Steve phoned.

'I'm sorry, Steve,' her mum said. 'It's awkward for us, and, most of all, awkward for your father. He'd be so embarrassed to meet either of us again. Please, let's just leave things for a while.'

Mallie went upstairs to bury herself in her duvet.

'Stupid old geezer,' she muttered into her pillow. 'He spoiled everything.'

Still, she couldn't forget the intense passion in the old man's face as he muttered, "Mrs H's picture."

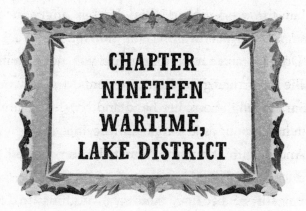

# CHAPTER
# NINETEEN
# WARTIME,
# LAKE DISTRICT

Tony and Mrs Cregg struggled through the milking next morning. Tony hadn't slept well. Between the old man's rasping cough, and thoughts of not being able to see Alice and Mrs H, he tossed sweatily in bed all night. As he hosed down the cowshed, he watched Mrs Cregg shoo the cows along the track to the pasture. She had made it quite clear that the after-milking clean-up job was his, which meant that there would be no chance of even a brief meeting with his friends this evening. It would be past nine o'clock by the time he'd finish.

He sighed, as he sloshed the water over the dung and watched it run in dirty rivulets into a channel through the cobbled yard. He felt tired at the thought of all the work ahead. And he felt angry at the thought of Alice waiting for him at the crooked tree. There was no way he could get word to her. She'd think badly of him. She and Mrs H would think him an ill-mannered idiot.

He stopped, and turned off the tap. He'd never keep up with this pace. Two jobs done – milking and cleaning – and he was already sinking into tired hopelessness, because there was nothing to look forward to except more dull chores.

He looked up at the sky and wondered about his father and Doris. What were they doing now? Did they really miss him, as they said in their letters? He'd prefer the nightly sirens – the rush to the basement and the tense listening to the droning planes with his father and Doris – to this wearisome existence. More than ever, he wanted to go home.

After four days of working from dawn until late evening, Tony was drained. His face was pale and there were dark circles under his eyes. If Doris could see him now, he thought, looking at himself in the foxed mirror over the scullery sink, she'd sort things out, just as she'd always sorted things out for him and Da. He kicked off the farm clogs and hurled them into a corner.

Mrs Cregg sensed his frustration as she ladled out yesterday's onion soup, with a few potatoes and parsley added to disguise it.

'I know you're tired, lad,' she said, pushing a loose strand of grey hair behind her ear. 'And so am I. But what can I do? Doctor says it's exhaustion and bronchitis, and insists Father stays in bed. We'll just have to do our best until he gets back on his feet. It won't be much longer.'

'Can't you hire somebody?' Tony asked. 'Even for a little while?'

Mrs Cregg frowned and shook her head. 'We can't afford it,' she said. 'Anyway, most of the young men around here have joined up.'

'Couldn't you ask a neighbour to help? Where I live, people help one another...'

'You city people just don't understand, do you?' said Mrs Cregg. 'Father and me, we keep to ourselves and don't bother anyone. Now, finish your supper, lad. Early rise in the morning.'

Tony leaned wearily on the table, his head resting

on his hands. How could he tell the old woman that he could take no more? Yet what could he do? If he ran away, she would have to do all the work on her own. He bit back his tears. He was stuck here like a rabbit in one of those awful snares.

In the distance, an aircraft hummed in the summer night.

'Blast this bloody war. Blast everything,' he whispered. 'I hate this war.'

'Me too, lad,' sighed Mrs Cregg. She got up to make sure the blackout curtains left no chinks. 'Them or ours?' she said. 'Never can tell, but we can't take chances.'

With the prospect of another hard day ahead, Tony half-wanted a bomb to fall right across the field – *BOOM!* – resulting in just enough injury, like a broken leg, to have him taken to a comfortable hospital where he'd have nothing to do but eat decent food and read comics and be fussed over.

Later, he bathed the blisters on his feet with cold water – he'd never quite broken in those clogs. He blew out his candle, drew back the curtains and leaned on the window ledge. Looking out over the moon-washed landscape, he weighed up his position. *I'm just a boy,* he thought. *I'm doing the work of a grown man for people who don't even want me here. But how can I leave the old woman to cope?* He sank his head into his folded arms, and sighed. *I don't belong here.*

Decision made, he climbed under the covers and gazed at the blue shadows of the window-frame that the moon was casting on the wooden floor. Criss-cross shadows, like prison bars.

Tomorrow he would leave this place.

# CHAPTER TWENTY

'Get a move on, Mallie Kelly,' shouted Ms Peabody in PE next day. 'Lift those feet and stop mooching around like a geriatric tortoise.'

'She has a headache, Miss,' said Jamila, springing to her friend's defence. 'I'll sit with her.'

'Headache?' muttered Mallie. 'I don't have a head—'

'Yes, you do,' insisted Jamila, pushing her pal on to a bench. 'Now, go with me on this. I have no great urge to work up a sweat – it ruins my hair. Are you still moping over the Steve thing? You're mad, you know. Daft as a sheep on crack. Snap out of it, Mal.'

'Can't,' said Mallie. 'Can't get it out of my head that old Armstrong recognised the picture. And there was me thinking that the same picture had brought good luck to Mum and me. I had such good vibes from it. So had Mum. I should've known.'

'Oh, that picture again!' groaned Jamila, giving an exaggerated yawn. 'Give it a rest, Mallie.'

'How can I?' protested Mallie. 'You weren't there to see the expression on the old man's face when he looked at it. I believe him, I really do. It probably seems like a small thing on the outside, but inside my head it's like a fire that won't go out. You wouldn't understand. Nobody would.'

'Look,' began Jamila. 'If it's that bad, why don't you go and see the man? Find out what happened – how the picture got into the antique shop.'

'Go and see him?' echoed Mallie. 'I'd rather put my head in a tiger's mouth.'

'Well, there *is* a faint chance that he'll feed you to the hamsters, but at least you'll die soft. Come on, Mallie. The worst that'll happen is that he'll refuse to talk and you'll go home knowing that you tried. End of story – and you can sleep at night. Go on like this, and you'll be a frazzled crone before you reach fifteen.'

Mallie gave a deep sigh as she rubbed her bare knees; it was cold in the hall. 'I suppose you're right,' she muttered. 'Keeping things bottled up inside your head only makes them grow into a monster that'll swallow you up. OK, I'll do it. Better if Steve is not there, though, he'd only complicate things. I need to see the old man on his own. In fact, today's the day Steve goes to the wholesale place to stock up on feed. He usually goes at around four-thirty for over an hour. I hate the thought of it, though, Jam. I'll get all tongue-tied.'

'Right,' said Jamila. 'I'll come with you for support.'

'No, Jamila,' put in Mallie quickly. 'I have to handle this myself. It has to be him and me.'

'Are you saying no?' said Jamila with mock horror. 'Afraid I'll end up being fed to the hamsters too?'

'No,' replied Mallie. 'I'm afraid you'll mouth off, and we'll all end up yelling.'

'Thanks.' Jamila laughed down the neck of her sweatshirt so that Ms Peabody wouldn't see. 'Now, will you please try to look like you're suffering and in need of my loving care. Vaulting over that heap of stuffed junk is so last-century.'

Mallie's mother wasn't in the house when she got

home. *Just as well*, thought Mallie. She knew Mum would block the proposed visit. She bit her lip as she took the picture from the dresser. She examined it, front and back, and wondered about its origin. She'd explain to Mum later. Mum would understand, once she'd calmed down.

Mallie took a bite from one of the sandwiches her mother had left out for her, and promptly spat it out. It was made up of bits of the leftover *Boeuf Stroganoff* with the sauce scraped off. They'd already had it under different guises for two lunches, a dinner and a supper.

She packed the picture into a supermarket bag and, with a sigh, pulled the front door shut behind her. She'd got as far as the gate when she met her mum. Mallie tried to look casual, but only succeeded in looking flustered.

'Where are you off to, Mallie?' her mum asked.

'Just… just,' Mallie stuttered. 'I'm just going down town for a minute. I'll be back soon.'

All the wrong words, of course – she knew that as soon as she'd uttered them. Her mum regarded her suspiciously.

'What are you up to? Pawning the family silver?' she laughed, pointing to the bag.

Mallie thrust the bag behind her back. 'It's nothing.'

Her mum screwed up her eyes. 'What is it, Mal? What are you up to?'

'Oh, look, Mum. Can't you just give over with the questions? Trust me.'

'I do. But why so secretive?' went on her mum.

'Mum, you're making a big fuss about nothing. Can't you just let me be?' She stood aside to let her mother pass.

Then: 'All right,' she said with an air of resignation. 'You win. I'll show you. Here,' she went on, taking the picture from the bag, 'this is what I'm doing, and I know you're going to shout me down. I'm taking this to old Mr Armstrong, OK? I can't stand the fact that he thinks I nicked it. And I know he recognised the picture, because he knows the words on the back. So, go on. Tell me I'm daft.'

Her mum stared thoughtfully at the picture for a few moments, then looked at the back of it. '*Mrs H's picture,*' she said. 'I know, you pointed that out to me before. Do you really think he's seen that at some time? Perhaps he took a look at it when…'

'No, Mum. I know he didn't. I was in the kitchen

all the time, so he couldn't have seen it earlier that evening.'

'OK,' said her mum, looking at the picture again. 'I think I understand.'

'You do?' Mallie breathed a sigh of relief. 'But that's it, Mum. I can't leave it be. I know he seems like a grumpy old fogey, but he's OK really. We were getting pally when this happened. I can't just ignore it.'

Her mum looked up from the picture and smiled. 'You're a good kid, Mal,' she said. 'Your heart is in the right place, even if your head is a tad soft. Sorry for being nosey.'

'It's all right,' muttered Mallie, taking the picture back. 'I suppose now you're going to tell me to forget it.'

'No,' said her mum. 'I'm not mad about the idea of you doing this – after all, you're the one who was wrongly accused. You go for it, Mal. OK, so you might get your head bitten off, but you'll come out the victor through your honesty. I think I should come with you. We'll sort it out together.'

Mallie raised her eyebrows. 'No, Mum,' she said. 'Promise you won't follow me. I've got to do this on my own.'

Her mum laughed. 'All right. Just don't take any crap, OK?'

'Huh, not me! If I'm not back in one hour, send out the posse.'

'Mallie!' Sarah called out, as Mallie walked away.

'Yes?'

'Where did I get a decent kid like you?'

Mallie smiled.

Just as Mallie turned the corner into High Street, she saw Steve getting into his minivan. She ducked into a shop doorway and waited until he'd driven to the end of the road. Then she braced herself and entered the shop.

# CHAPTER
# TWENTY-ONE

Mr Armstrong was bent over an aquarium, leaning on his stick and slowly dropping food in to the darting goldfish with his other hand. He was talking to them in an affectionate tone of voice. Mallie stood at the door, not quite sure of her next move.

Mr Armstrong straightened up. He frowned, when he saw who it was. They regarded one another for a moment.

'Well. Come to gloat at the disgraced old man, then?' he said.

Mallie's nervousness disappeared in a flash of annoyance. 'Rude as ever,' she said. 'I'm not the gloating type, Mr Armstrong. I would have thought you'd know that by now. I've come to talk to you, but if you're just going to insult me, I might as well leave.'

'No, wait,' said Mr Armstrong, his expression lifting. 'Don't go, Mallie. I... I didn't mean... '

'Like you didn't mean it when you called me a thief?' said Mallie.

'I'm really sorry,' went on Mr Armstrong, waving her into the shop. 'Let's start again.'

Mallie frowned defensively. 'OK,' she muttered, and she slowly advanced. 'But you growl at me once more, and I'm gone.' She stood before Mr Armstrong and they eyed one another warily.

'Well, where do we go from here?' said Mr Armstrong in his forthright way. 'Do you want your job back? Steve isn't here just now, but I'll be glad for you to come back. I miss you...'

'Actually, it's not about that,' Mallie took a deep breath. 'I've come to ask you about this.' She eased the picture from the plastic bag and held it out.

Mr Armstrong looked at the picture. 'Mrs H's picture,' he murmured. 'It really is Mrs H's picture. I thought I'd lost it years ago. Where did you get – find it?'

'In an antique shop,' said Mallie. 'And, before you ask, Mr Armstrong, I've no idea how it got there.'

His face softened as he looked at the back and ran a finger over the tatty label.

'Sit down, Mallie,' he said, pulling out a stool for her and a chair for himself. 'I wrote that,' he said eventually, 'when I was ten.' He was silent for a moment. Then: 'That girl was the best friend I ever had, even though I only knew her for a few months.' He lapsed into silence as he gazed at the picture of the girl with the rabbit.

Mallie sat patiently as the old man let his memories wash over him. After a few moments he blinked, and looked at her.

'It was during the war, you see,' he began. 'Hitler's war,' he added. 'I was the loneliest child you could imagine. Then I met Alice.'

Just then, a customer came into the shop. As Mr Armstrong leaned on his stick and went to deal with him, Mallie looked at the picture and tried to imagine the old man as a child, friendly with this little girl. But her imagination failed. To her, he was still an old man.

When the customer left, Mr Armstrong came back and told Mallie about his Irish father and coming to

London at the age of five.

'Rabbits,' he smiled. 'All I wanted was a house with a garden and a hutch for rabbits – ever since the time when I was very small and my mother and I used to fantasise over a picture of rabbits. But I ended up in a one-room flat with a collection of tin animals. They went with me wherever I went. Even when the bombs fell around us, and when I was sent away as an evacuee, those tin animals were first to be packed. I suppose I knew even then that I wanted a life with real animals.'

'You were sent away during the war?' said Mallie. 'I read about that, but I've never met anyone who went away. What was it like?'

'Lonely at first,' Mr Armstrong replied.

Between serving customers, he told Mallie about meeting Alice and life with the Creggs, in 'a beautiful, peaceful place – Lake Windermere. Even the name still fills me with emotion.' He looked at Mallie, as if he was afraid she'd scoff.

'Go on,' she said gently.

'Good people,' Mr Armstrong sighed, 'though they expected a bit much from a young lad. Then I met her,' he went on, pointing to the picture. 'Alice. She brightened my life, she and Mrs H.'

'Who was Mrs H?'

The old man shook his head and smiled. 'Do you know, I never found out what her full name was. Alice always called her Mrs H, so I did too. I used to meet them every evening after the milking. We'd walk through the fields and woods. Mrs H taught us so much about animals and nature. She showed us how to fix broken wings and small-animal legs, and how to take ticks from field mice. Then we'd go back to Mrs H's place and have tea and American biscuits. And music,' he added with a smile. 'One special evening we had music.'

'You mean, she played the piano?' asked Mallie.

'No. Alice had some records that had belonged to her father. Jazz records. Like me with my tin animals, she took her records everywhere. I suppose we were both clinging to something that made us feel secure. She was always telling Mrs H and me about her records. So much so, that Mrs H told her to bring her "wretched records" and she could play them on an old record player that had belonged to Mrs H's mother.'

'So she brought them?'

Mr Armstrong nodded and smiled. 'It was one of the few occasions we were allowed into the house.

Though it wasn't where she actually lived. She had another house nearby, but she loved to come and just sit outside her old home in the evenings. Never told us much about herself, but she loved to listen to us. I remember the way she pretended to be appalled by Duke Ellington's music. Then she laughed, and said her mother would turn in her grave if she thought there was jazz playing on her old gramophone. Somehow she got great satisfaction out of that. I think Mrs H's mother was a bit of a cold individual, from the odd remark she dropped.'

'So that's where you got your taste for old jazz?'

'Yes,' he nodded. 'We played them over and over again that evening. Good times, Mallie. Even though there was a war raging, we were cocooned up there in the Lake District, me and Mrs H and Alice.'

'So you were happy there during the war?' said Mallie.

Mr Armstrong shook his head. 'Until I decided to run away,' he said.

'Why did you want to do that? Go back to the bombs and terror? You must have been mad.'

'Not mad,' explained Mr Armstrong. 'Tired and lonely.'

'I thought you said...'

'Let me finish, girl.' And Mr Armstrong went on to tell Mallie about how hard it had been when Mr Cregg got ill, and he could no longer go to see Alice and Mrs H.

'It got too much, so I packed my things,' he said. 'Hid them in the cowshed, and after the milking one morning, I legged it. Excuse me.' He left to deal with a couple of customers. Mallie looked at the old man and felt a strange sympathy – even though she knew nothing of war or of hardship. She waited impatiently for the customers to leave.

'All the way back to London?' she asked, when he came back.

He shook his head. 'I only got a few miles – as far as a village called Near Sawrey,' he said. 'I met Alice outside the grocery store. First she ticked me off for being out of touch for so long. Then, when she heard my side of the story, she hauled me along to Mrs H's other place. Literally hauled me,' he laughed. 'She took my arm and wouldn't let go. Well, to cut a long story short, Mrs H sent one of her farmhands over to the Creggs to help out.'

'So you had more time to spend with your friends,' said Mallie. 'A decent sort, that Mrs H.'

'You don't know the half of it,' said Mr Armstrong.

'I learnt so much about life from that lady in the short time I was there. And from Alice too. We were so... so right together, the three of us.'

'Did you stay there for the whole war?' asked Mallie.

Mr Armstrong sighed, then he frowned at her. 'Are you just being polite, or what? You don't have to listen to this, you know. You can't possibly be interested in things that happened years ago.'

It was Mallie's turn to frown. 'There you go again,' she said. 'Always suspicious, that's you. I wonder what that girl saw in you. I'd certainly have run a mile from a boy like you if you were anything like as grumpy as you are now. As it happens, I *am* interested.'

The old man laughed. 'Grumpy, eh? How right you are, missy. Maybe "defensive" is a better word. I learned to put up a shield against the things life threw at me.'

'A shield also keeps out the good things, you know,' said Mallie gently.

The old man nodded. 'I know,' he said. 'I know that now, even though it's a bit late in the day.'

'Never too late for change,' said Mallie.'

'Well, aren't you the philosophical young madam,'

laughed Mr Armstrong. 'But you're absolutely right. Look,' he added, making a brushing movement in front of his face. 'No shield.'

'Anyway,' Mallie went on, 'I suppose all this is leading up to the picture, and that's why I'm here. Please go on.'

Mr Armstrong laughed again. 'That's exactly the sort of thing Alice would have said. She was a feisty madam, just like you. Maybe that's why I tolerate you,' he added, with a mischievous glint in his eyes.

Mallie smiled. 'What about the picture?'

'Ah, the picture,' Mr Armstrong took it up again and gazed at it. 'It was shortly after Mrs H's farmhand began working for the Creggs. I went over to Mrs H's house – the one with the porch. It was one of those balmy days in late summer, I remember. Mrs H was sitting in a basket chair, a big floppy hat on her head. She had a sketchbook on her knee and she was drawing a picture of Alice holding a rabbit we'd freed from a snare a few days before. I'm so pleased to have it back.'

# CHAPTER TWENTY-TWO

Mallie looked at the picture with renewed interest. Suddenly it had become real.

'I stopped just before I reached them,' went on Mr Armstrong. 'Mrs H called out to me, asked me why I'd stopped. I tried to tell her that I wished I could keep the image in my head always.' He stopped and looked at Mallie. 'Does that sound strange?'

Mallie shook her head and said nothing. She didn't want to interrupt the small-boy feelings that were being revived in the old man.

He laughed gently and continued. 'Mrs H got up and went into the house. I thought I'd offended her.

But she came back with a box camera that she said had belonged to her father. Apparently he'd been a keen photographer. I couldn't believe it when she handed it to me and said I could take a picture with it. I was thrilled. Then, when she started sketching Alice again, I took a photo of Alice and the rabbit.'

'Really?' put in Mallie. 'You have a photo of them?'

Mr Armstrong shook his head. "I gave the camera back to Mrs H. She said she would have the film developed in the village. She very kindly lent me the drawing so that I could "keep the image in my head" until the film was developed, and then I was to give the drawing to Alice.'

'And did you?'

The old man paused and looked at the picture again. 'No,' he began. 'When I arrived back at the Creggs later that day, Mrs Cregg met me with a grim face...'

'The old bat,' muttered Alice. 'She didn't want you having fun.'

'Nothing like that,' said Mr Armstrong. 'She told me I had a visitor...'

'A visitor! Who?'

'Will you let me get on with my story?' he said. 'That is, if you're sure you still want to hear an old man's ramblings.'

'Sorry. Go on.'

'The visitor was Doris. She was sitting there in the parlour. I remember how she got up as I ran to her – I was absolutely thrilled that she'd come all this way to see me – and she put her hands on my shoulders. I suppose I should have known something was wrong. It was my father. A bomb had fallen on the garage where he worked in Kilburn.'

'Oh no,' whispered Alice.

'Killed instantly. That ended my stay in the Lake District. Doris took me back for my father's funeral. Stop looking at me with pity in your eyes, Mallie. It was wartime. Death happened all the time.'

'And you stop being so matter-of-fact about it,' said Mallie. 'That was so awful. You must have been in bits.'

'Numb,' said Mr Armstrong. 'Just numb. I don't even remember the journey back to London. There you have it. That's my story and the story of this picture. I kept it all these years, but when I moved here, I couldn't find it. I figured it must have got lost in the move.'

'Or been stolen by me,' Mallie said with a wry

grin. 'Anyway, I thought you said you only had the picture on loan from Alice. Why didn't you give it back to her?'

'I never saw her again,' replied Mr Armstrong, stretching out his injured leg and rubbing his knee. 'I never went back.'

'Why not?' asked Mallie.

'By the time I could afford the journey, it was many years after the war. I knew there would be many changes, and I wanted to remember the place as it had been. I was sure Mrs H would be dead – she was quite old even when I knew her. I didn't want to see her place with other people living there. And I knew Alice would have gone back to London after the war.' He shrugged and looked at Mallie. 'I just wanted to remember them both as they were. Can you understand that?'

'I think so,' said Mallie. 'I have foggy memories of my father. But I mostly think of him as someone who gave me piggy-backs, took me on long, chatty walks and read books to me. I don't want to be shown the hole in the ground where he is now. Same with my granny. They were both killed in a car accident. She was an artist, like Mum. Great at drawing small animals. But Mum packed away all her art and stuff in the attic. She never really came to terms with those deaths. I've never told anyone that before,' she added.

'Well, that's two things we have in common,' said Mr Armstrong. 'I haven't done much talking about my war. None, in fact, until now.'

'What about Steve?' asked Mallie. 'Surely you told your son…'

Mr Armstrong leaned towards her. 'I've only really been getting to know Steve recently,' he said. 'His mother and I split up when Steve was nine. He was brought up in Wales by his mother. I had him to stay sometimes during school holidays. Apart from that…' He shrugged.

Mallie looked shocked.

'It was for the best,' replied Mr Armstrong. 'I'm a bit of a loner. That infernal shield,' he added, with an embarrassed laugh. 'It was better that he should have the love and affection of his mother than be torn between two incompatible people. Of course, I supported him,' he added. 'I put him through college, and all that. He helped me to set up this shop before he went out into the world – I'm too crocked now to practise fully as a vet. Giving advice to people with small animals suits me fine.'

'Didn't you even write to one another?' asked Mallie.

'Sporadically. He's been away for years, but we always kept in touch, especially after his mother died. As soon as he starts his lecturing job, he'll be given a house. But he'll be near enough. Now, don't you think you've heard enough? What is it about you, Mallie Kelly, that you've loosened an old man's memories? You must be bored mindless.'

'What about Doris?' asked Mallie, ignoring his remark. 'What became of her?'

'Doris?' Mr Armstrong said. 'Doris took me under her wing – well, that was nothing new. She'd always been a surrogate mother to me. She got married a few years later and had a family of her own.'

'That must have made you happy.' Mallie said hopefully, 'having a family.'

'They weren't really my family. Anyway, there was such a huge age-gap. After all, I was sixteen when her first child arrived. Oh, don't get me wrong. Doris was kind and loving – and I loved her too. But I still felt separate. She and her husband helped put me through vet college. After that, I went my own way. We kept in touch for a while. Then it was just Christmas cards and the odd letter until Doris died at seventy-three. And here I am now – a charmingly sweet old man.'

'Yeah, right,' laughed Mallie. 'Just one thing, though.'

'Oh? And what's that?'

'How did that picture get into Bert's antique shop?'

'I can't think...' began Mr Armstrong. But before he could continue, the door flew open and Mallie's mum rushed in.

'Mum!' groaned Mallie. 'You promised you'd let me handle this on my own!'

Sarah Kelly was flushed and agitated. 'That picture,' she began. 'Where is it? Show me. Please.'

Mr Armstrong stood up, leaned on his stick and instinctively put his other hand protectively over the picture.

'Mum!' Mallie said again.

Her mum sat down on a sack of dog food and gasped to catch her breath. She leaned forward to look at the picture in Mr Armstrong's hand.

'I should have known,' she said quietly. 'I should have remembered.'

'What do you mean, Mum?' asked Mallie.

'This,' said Sarah. She took a small, tissue paper package from her bag and unwrapped it. Without a word she handed it to Mr Armstrong.

He gasped.

'What is it?' cried Mallie. 'What's going on, Mum?'

Mr Armstrong sat down and handed what was in the tissue paper to Mallie.

'It's a photo! A photo of the girl with the rabbit!' She looked across at her mother, who was still breathless.

'It's Alice,' put in Mr Armstrong, taking the photo back and holding it side-by-side with the framed drawing. 'That's the photo I took! The one I was telling you about, Mallie. This is my friend Alice. Mary Alice, as she often told me when she was being formal,' he laughed.

'That's my name!' said Mallie. 'I'm Mary Alice too. I don't understand. What's going on here? Mum, how come you have this photo?'

'That's your granny, Mal,' said Sarah, leaning against the desk. 'My mother, Mary Alice. She was so pleased when I named you after her.'

'I can't believe this,' exclaimed Mallie. 'Are

you telling me that Granny was the Alice who was Mr Armstrong's friend in the war?'

'That seems to be it,' said Mr Armstrong. 'I'm as puzzled as you, Mallie,' he went on, looking questioningly at Sarah.

'I should have remembered,' put in Sarah. 'I knew there was something niggling me about that picture. A sort of *déjà-vu*. Remember, Mallie? That time you gave it to me. And you thought I was putting on an act? It was just now, when I met you at the gate this morning, that something prompted me to look through my mother's things in the attic. And here we are,' she added, gesturing at the two pictures.

She looked at Mr Armstrong as if she was seeing him for the first time.

'My mother never talked much about the war, Mr Armstrong,' she said. 'She was a feisty lady who got on with life. But she did tell me something about her time as an evacuee in the Lake District. She said it was the happiest time of her life. I remember, I scoffed at that and asked how a war could have been happy. But she would just smile, and retreat into her memories.'

Mr Armstrong was nodding his head in agreement. 'I know,' he said. 'I know exactly how she felt.'

# CHAPTER
# TWENTY-THREE

There were trucks and vans all around the Castle grounds, and a smell of damp grass. Mallie and Jamila were ushered, along with a group of others, into a big marquee. All around them, chattering loudly, were people holding plastic-wrapped pictures, figurines, ornaments, dolls and every sort of pottery, silver and boxes. Farther away, in another marquee, old furniture and large statues were being carried in and set up.

The rain dripped down the back of Mallie's neck, and her feet squelched in the new sandals she'd bought with her own money. She wished she hadn't come. There were so many people.

Yet there was an air of camaraderie mixed with anticipation and excitement.

'Well, at least we're out of that downpour,' laughed a woman in a flowery dress, cradling a brass urn against her cushiony bosom.

Mallie nodded, and wiped her wet face with her sleeve. 'This was a stupid idea,' she whispered to Jamila. 'Look at all the stuff other people have, Jam. It's far more interesting than mine. I'm going to feel a right nellie.'

'Oh, don't be such a moaner, Mallie,' said Jamila. 'Isn't it lucky I read the newspapers? The Antiques Roadshow here at the Castle. Imagine – the Antiques Roadshow! For real! I just knew your picture would be perfect to bring along.'

'Are you sure?'

'Of course I'm sure, Mal. Besides, we're surrounded by cameramen and guys shoving woolly microphones into people's faces. We could get lucky, maybe get discovered. That's how a lot of celebs get started. Someone spots them and then, hey – it's big spreads in the glossies, and before they know it they're doing the red carpet thing. This is *exciting*. Here, you want some of my lip gloss?'

'It's OK for you,' muttered Mallie, dipping her little finger into Jamila's lip gloss. 'I'm the one who has to do the talking. What if they tell me this is just pretty junk? What if the camera focuses in on me when they laugh and tell me that? I'll die. Why don't we leave now?'

'Too late,' laughed Jamila. 'Look, they're getting people in line. Anyway, it's bucketing down outside. I'm damned if I'm going to get my hair messed up. Get *him*!' she cried, as a young man with a clipboard approached them.

'Pictures this way,' he said. 'Anyone with oil paintings, watercolours, engravings – anything framed – please follow me.'

Mallie hung back. 'I don't think I want to do this,' she muttered.

'No way,' laughed Jamila, clutching her friend's arm. 'Where that guy goes, Jamila goes. Come on. It'll be fun. Now, tell me again what happened when your mum barged in.'

'I've told you,' said Mallie, as they followed the young man through the drizzle into another marquee.

'I know, but I want to hear it again. Go on, we'll be ages queuing here. What did you think when your mum barged in?'

'I nearly died,' said Mallie, with an air of resignation. 'I was so sure she was going to make a big fuss. Then Mum explained that she'd always had a feeling of *déja vu* about the drawing. It wasn't until she looked at it again, when I was heading off to talk to Mr Armstrong, that she thought she recognised it. She went up to the attic where my granny's stuff is stored, and found the photo in an album.'

'How weird was that!' put in Jamila. 'Imagine – all the time it was your granny.'

'I know,' laughed Mallie. 'Mr Armstrong shut the shop – it was nearly closing time, anyway – and took us through to his sitting-room. He showed us the tin animals he'd had since he was a kid, and he showed us other photos he'd taken with the camera Mrs H had given him. Animals and scenery, mostly.

'Funny, isn't it,' she went on, 'two kids from the streets of London with the same love for animals that they only knew from pictures up to then. Mrs H encouraged them. Mr Armstrong said that she used to tell him and my granny that they could be anything they wanted to be. She told them that if they had enough passion running through their veins, they'd find a way to fulfil their dreams.

And they did. He became a vet, and my granny became an artist. Mrs H encouraged her to draw. Mum told me that when Granny went back to London after the war – she lived with a woman who treated her like a skivvy – she worked hard to get a scholarship to art school, and took off. That's where my mum got her talent for drawing animals. Except that Mum, being the stubborn creature that she is, fought against what she was good at, just to be different from her mother.'

'Did your granny ever talk about Mrs H?' asked Jamila.

'Don't remember,' replied Mallie, kicking at a damp clump of grass.

'That's sad,' put in Jamila, 'that she didn't end up hooked to old Mr Armstrong.'

'Oh, look, Jam,' Mallie interrupted. 'There's that famous guy. The one who talks about pictures.'

She shrank back as they drew nearer to the familiar faces of the experts at the end of the marquee. Here there were lights on long poles, cameras poised for action and flexes like thick spaghetti snaking around the marquee. The atmosphere was electric. Anyone who got this far was bound to be interviewed.

How could she have allowed herself to be talked into this?

'Why couldn't you have picked on some junk from your own house, Jam?' Mallie muttered. 'God knows, there's plenty of it.'

Jamila laughed. 'We needed something classy, Mal. You have to agree, that picture is special. It has a story to it. These people like something with a bit of a story – it's what makes good television. Who wants to hear about some old Chinese urn or a Victorian chamber-pot unless it has a story?'

'Story? I'm not going to tell them the story.'

'Name, please.'

Mallie blinked dumbly at the businesslike woman who was peering at her.

'Her name is Mary Alice Kelly, and I'm her friend, Jamila.'

'Mallie. My name is Mallie,' Mallie scowled at her pal. How would she get through, knowing that millions of people would be watching? That is, if her item was chosen for the show. Just a nice drawing, worth zilch. A big laugh. Now would be a good time to break away and tell them not to bother, thank you very much.

'This way, Mallie,' said the woman, propelling her

gently towards the table where a man in a suit was sitting. He smiled, and indicated the chairs beside him. There were people all around looking curiously at them.

As the two girls sat down, Jamila gave Mallie's hand an encouraging squeeze. The lights were on, the cameras were rolling!

'Well, what have we here?' The man said, holding out his hand.

Jamila nudged her. 'Go on, Mal,' she whispered. 'Show him.'

Mallie swallowed hard and handed over the plastic supermarket bag. She watched, as the man eased the picture from the bag. He peered at it, turned it over and read the label on the back.

*'Mrs H's picture,'* he read. Mallie nodded.

'No signature,' he went on.

'No,' mumbled Mallie.

'Good, though, isn't it?' said Jamila.

The man nodded. 'It's very good. Would you mind if I remove the frame? It's an amateur frame, and sometimes frames like this conceal a signature.'

Mallie shrugged. 'I suppose so,' she said. She'd come this far, so she might as well go the whole hog. She tried not to look at the camera in case she lost her nerve completely. *It's just a short interview,* she thought. *I'm just having a chat with this man. No worries.*

Very gently, the man unwrapped the ancient passepartout binding the picture to the glass. The margin that had been covered was white against the rest of the picture. He peered at the drawing. Then he held it away from him to see it from a different angle.

'Ah,' he said. 'Just as I thought. A signature... Oh, my goodness,' he added. 'What have we here?'

He peered even closer. Then he looked up at Mallie.

'Have you any idea? I mean, do you know what this picture is? This is...' He was shaking his head and smiling.

The people behind leaned closer.

# CHAPTER
# TWENTY-FOUR

'Where did you get this?' he asked.

'Mallie's granny,' said Jamila. 'Her granny is the girl in the picture. She was a… what's the word, Mallie?'

'An evacuee,' said Mallie, now nervous because of the man's reaction. 'She was an evacuee somewhere in the Lake District during the war. She got friendly with the woman who drew the picture – Mrs H.'

'Do you know who Mrs H was?' the man asked, still peering at the signature.

By now, the cameraman had moved closer to get a clear image of the picture. Mallie bit her lip.

'Mrs Heelis, that's who,' the picture expert went on.

Mallie was suddenly conscious of the camera focused on her.

'Do you know who Mrs Heelis was?' the man went on.

'Stop teasing, and tell us,' put in Jamila.

'Beatrix Potter,' the man said dramatically. 'See her signature here? *HBP 1941.* Those are the initials of Helen Beatrix Potter.'

There was a stunned silence. Mallie stared at him, her mouth open.

'Have you any idea what this drawing is worth?'

Mallie shook her head again, doubtful that she'd heard properly.

'Well, you'll want to insure it. This is a real gem – an original sketch by Beatrix Potter in her old age.'

'I don't believe it,' Mallie gasped.

'What?' said Jamila impatiently, eyeing the camera. 'You mean the woman who did little books about animals? Mrs Tiggy-Winkle and Peter Rabbit and all that? My brother loves them.'

'Jam,' said Mallie, 'years and years ago, Beatrix Potter was *the* most famous children's writer. She wrote and illustrated loads of books about little animals. I just don't believe this.' She looked at the man to see if he was kidding.

'Believe it,' he said. 'There's her signature – *HBP 1941*. Two years before she died. This is an important picture you have here.'

'Tell him, Mallie,' prompted Jamila. 'Tell him about it. I told you it was an interesting story.'

With nudges and prompts from Jamila, and trying not to let the camera intimidate her, Mallie struggled through the story of Mary Alice and Tony, the two evacuees who had never known they were in the presence of the famous Beatrix Potter.

'That would be typical of her in her old age,' the expert said. 'She played down her fame so that the youngsters wouldn't be overawed by her importance.'

'Mum said that her mother used to talk about an old lady – a sheep farmer – who encouraged her to draw,' said Mallie.

'Perhaps it was just as well,' the man said, 'that your granny remembered her as a friend who encouraged her, rather than as a well-known personality. This is an amazing find. But I don't suppose you'll want to sell it, since it's a family heirloom?'

Mallie smiled. 'They don't even know I've brought it here,' she confessed.

The man laughed. 'Well, they'll know soon enough,

when this programme goes out,' he said.

'You mean you're going to use it?' asked Jamila, settling her plait and working her face into her much-practised glam look. 'We're going to be on telly, Mallie,' she whispered, nudging her pal. 'We're in!'

🐇🐇

As they made their way out of the Castle grounds, Mallie was still in a daze.

'Imagine,' she said. 'My granny was matey with Beatrix Potter! I still can't believe it. Wait until I tell Mum. It was hard enough for her to cope with us finding Gran's Tony, but to find out she spent part of the war with Beatrix Potter – wow!'

'Aren't you glad, Mal, that I made you buy that picture instead of jewellery?' laughed Jamila. She ducked, as Mallie reached out to slap her.

'Come on,' said Mallie. 'Wait till we tell Mum and Steve and Mr Armstrong. They'll die of excitement. Beatrix Potter!'

'Are you sure the old man won't mind that you took his picture along? Won't he think you've stolen it for real?' began Jamila.

Mallie stopped. 'This precious item,' she said,

holding the plastic bag aloft, 'belongs to *me*. Mr Armstrong said that, because it was always on loan to him, he was delighted to be able to return it to Mary Alice via me – another Mary Alice. What a story, Jam! Better than any of your aunty's romances.'

'Great,' said Jamila. 'Now, where are we meeting?'

'At Chez Hans,' laughed Mallie, looking at her watch. 'This time it'll be a proper meal. French and posh and Steve's treat. Just promise that you won't do any of your romantic match-making stuff in front of my mum and Steve. Especially since poor old Steve is trying to make up for causing all this trouble.'

'What trouble?'

'Oh, didn't I tell you?' Mallie giggled. 'When he was helping to move the old man to his new home, he put what he thought was just a load of junk into a box and left it all to be put up for auction. The picture was there in the box – he hadn't even looked at it.'

'Enter Bert's Antiques and Bric-a-Brac,' laughed Jamila. 'That's karma, Mallie. The signs are good.'

'Get away, Jam. There you go again with your schmaltzy lovey-dovey crap. Look, they're talking, Mum and Steve. In fact they're off getting estimates for printing cards and calendars to sell in the pet shop. Mum got the idea when she was showing Steve and his dad her mother's stuff.'

'She did?' said Jamila, with a knowing gleam in her eyes. 'She's softening, Mallie, I'm telling you.'

'And I'm telling you that it's purely business,' laughed Mallie.

Mr Armstrong, Steve and Sarah were already seated in the bar attached to the restaurant when the girls joined them. They were examining the menu.

'Good timing, girls,' said Sarah. 'Our table will be ready fairly soon.'

'Ah, Mallie and her minder,' joked Mr Armstrong. 'Come along, ladies, let's raise a glass to our new business venture. Sparkling water with a dash of lime,' he whispered to Mallie, as she sat down beside him. 'So no wild talk from the old man, see?'

Mallie grinned. 'Maybe it's my turn to do the wild talk,' she whispered back.

'What do you mean?' asked Mr Armstrong.

Mallie put the plastic bag down on the table and gently drew out the picture. She handed it to Mr Armstrong.

'Why are you giving it to me, Mallie?' he said. 'I've already told you that it's yours. Oh, you've taken the frame off.'

'Just read the signature on the back,' replied Mallie.

Mr Armstrong turned the picture over. 'HBP Nineteen-forty-one,' he read out. Then he shrugged his shoulders and looked at Mallie.

'What did you say, Mr Armstrong?' put in Sarah.

'HBP,' he said. 'Nineteen forty-one.'

'Never,' gasped Sarah. 'I don't believe it.' She got up and stood behind Mr Armstrong. 'My goodness,' she whispered, leaning closer to the picture. 'Beatrix Potter. Mrs H – your friend during the war – was Beatrix Potter.'

'What?' asked Steve.

'We've been to the Antiques Roadshow,' put in Mallie. 'That's how we found out. They're filming at the Castle. The expert was flabbergasted. He said it was definitely by Beatrix Potter.'

'Oh my!' said Sarah. 'This is just... amazing. Go on, tell us more.'

'The picture expert took the frame off and found the signature,' said Mallie. 'Imagine, Mr Armstrong! You and my granny were friendly with Beatrix Potter!'

'Really?' Mr Armstrong peered more closely at the picture. 'The famous Beatrix Potter? Good heavens.'

'Beatrix Potter!' exclaimed Steve. Then he put his hands over his face and gave an exaggerated groan.

'Pardon me while I crawl away, folks. To think I put it in with the junk!'

Sarah laughed, and put her hand on his shoulder. 'Well, think again, Steve,' she said softly. 'If you hadn't done what you did, none of us would be here now celebrating a new business and new friendship.'

'I'll drink to that,' laughed Mr Armstrong, raising his glass of sparkling water. 'To friendship,' he said, looking at everyone around the table. 'This is good. This is very good.' He beamed. 'And a special thanks to the generous old lady who let two troubled youngsters into her life.'

Mallie smiled and raised her glass. 'And to rabbits!'

# BEATRIX POTTER
# (1866-1943)

Beatrix Potter was born to well-to-do parents in London in 1866. As was the fashion of the time, her mother had little to do with the baby, entrusting her to the care of a strict nurse. For the rest of her life, Mrs Potter was a distant and unaffectionate mother. As a little girl, Beatrix's lonely existence was relieved by reading. She was particularly inspired by Sir John Tenniel's illustrations for Lewis Carroll's *Alice in Wonderland*, and throughout her childhood and adolescence she filled dozens of sketchbooks with detailed drawings of animals, flowers, house interiors and landscapes. Rupert Potter, Beatrix's father, a talented amateur photographer, was friendly with the painter John Everett Millais and often took Beatrix to visit his studio, where she learnt to mix colours. Her fondness for rabbits began with Benjamin Bouncer, the first of many pet rabbits that she drew – which eventually became the Mopsy, Topsy, Cottontail and Peter of her famous illustrated letter to a young, sick friend. This led to her charming series of little books published by Frederick Warne.

Beatrix's love for the countryside came initially from her visits to the Potter grandparents' rambling house, Camfield, in Hertfordshire. In the 1880s and 1890s the family began taking their annual summer holidays in the Lake District, and it was here that Beatrix discovered the place she came to love best. In 1905, with the money she earned from her books, she bought Hill Top farm and began breeding her beloved Herdwick sheep. In 1913 she married William Heelis and moved to nearby Castle Cottage. But Beatrix held on to Hill Top and divided her time between both houses.

Although she liked children, they were rarely allowed into her house.

Because of her difficult relationship with her mother, Beatrix would have got quite a kick out of playing Alice's jazz on the oh-so-precious gramophone.

# SOURCES

*The Home Front*, Peter Caddick-Adams,
www.bbc.co.uk/history/trail/wars_conflict/
home_front

*Beatrix Potter Artist, Storyteller and Countrywoman*,
Judy Taylor (Warne, 1996).

*Beatrix Potter: At Home in the Lake District*,
Susan Denyer (Frances Lincoln in association with
the National Trust, 2000).

# ACKNOWLEDGEMENTS

The author wishes to thank Tina Morton,
Borough Archivist, Brent Archive; Alex Sydney,
Head of Heritage Services, London Borough of Brent;
and the National Trust for research carried out at
Hill Top and at the Beatrix Potter Gallery, Cumbria;
and Sue Rosen, Camden Local Studies and
Archives Centre. Love and thanks to my husband
Emmet for his excellent help, sound advice
and welcome cups of coffee. And special thanks
to my editor, Yvonne Whiteman.

MARY ARRIGAN lives in County Tipperary in an old house between an isolated 12th-century abbey, a creepy forest and a peat bog. No surprise, then, that many of her teenage books are scary, though with a dash of humour. However, *Esty's Gold*, her previous book for Frances Lincoln, was inspired by the Irish Famine Museum and a trip to Ballarat, Australia. Her hobbies are tennis, books, crosswords, walking with Ossie the dog and having fun with her family. Her books have been translated into many languages, and her awards include The Sunday Times CWA Award, International White Ravens, Munich, The Hennessy Literary Short Story Award and the Bisto Merit Award.

## ESTY'S GOLD
Mary Arrigan

Esty's childhood world is shattered when her father is killed
defending starving Irish peasants. Suddenly forced to leave
home and work as a maid, it is only the dream of gold and
a better life in Australia that keeps her going. With stubborn
determination, she gets her family to the goldfields of
Ballarat. There, harsh conditions, deceit and rebellion
threaten to thwart them... but nothing is going to
destroy Esty's dream.

This gripping adventure story by an award-winning
Irish writer tells a timeless tale of hope and courage.

"Mary Arrigan always keeps her readers
agog with cracking adventures."
*Irish Times*

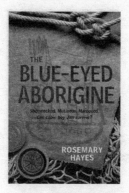

## THE BLUE-EYED ABORIGINE
### Rosemary Hayes

It is 1629, and there is mutiny in the air aboard the Dutch
ship Batavia as she plies her way towards Java with her
precious cargo. Jan, a cabin boy, and Wouter, a young soldier,
find themselves caught up in the tragic wrecking and bloody
revolt that follow. But worse is to come…

Based on real events, Rosemary Hayes's gripping story
recaptures some of sea history's most dramatic moments,
linking the fates of Jan and Wouter with discoveries
that intrigue Australians to this day.

"A definite must-read." *Young Writers*

"Gives an excellent account of the wrecking of the Batavia
whilst telling a captivating tale." *ReadPlus*

"Intriguing, hard-hitting story." *Reading Upside Down*

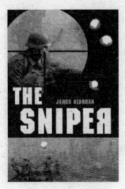

**THE SNIPER**
James Riordan

Stalingrad snipers were a legend in their time.
Their patience, keen eyes and ruthlessness helped win the
Battle of Stalingrad and turn the tide of the Second World
War. This is the true story of a teenage sniper recruited in
1942 by Vasily Zaitsev to seek out and shoot German
officers. To begin with, the youngster finds it almost
impossible to kill, but after a shocking discovery, goes on to
'snap as many as 84 German sticks', and following capture
and a daredevil escape, leads a handpicked unit on a
hazardous mission – to seize Field Marshall Paulus, the
Commander-in-Chief of the invading army.

But this sniper is no ordinary marksman...

"A powerful and heart-rending story." *School Librarian*

"I for one could not put the book down." *IBBY Link*